Seven Rabbits
By Timothy King

<u>Trigger</u>
<u>Warning</u>

Violence against women

    Sexual assault

    Extreme acts of violence

    Suicide

    Torture

    And overall, rough shit

If you or someone you know is struggling with thoughts of suicide, please call the National Suicide Hotline by dialing 988.

If you or someone you know is a victim of domestic violence, please call the National Domestic Violence Hotline by dialing 800-799-7233.

BY TIMOTHY KING

<u>Dedication</u>

For my wife, who always supports my crazy dreams
And my parents for teaching me to love reading

Special Thanks

A Special Thank You to my editor: Heather Ann Larson

And to my Beta readers: Ali Sweet, Dallis Jensen, Aneka Bailey, and Laura Bilodeau

You helped my dreams come true.

Contents

Chapter 1

Chase Rogers peered out the window of his father's Chevy, watching rows of trees zip past. His black duffel bag lay in his lap, embroidered with his name, jersey number, and the high school mascot. His family moved to Tall Oak eight months ago from Tampa. Although Tall Oak was still in Florida, it felt like a different country. Tampa was one of the fastest-growing cities in the United States, while Tall Oak was a dying town with one thing going for it - high school football.

"Number eighty-eight, you good?" his father asked, a hint of concern in his voice.

Chase looked at his father. The man moved them to Tall Oak for a factory job. The same factory that closed down two months after their move. Stress lines creased the older man's face. Despite the pressure he must have been under, he tried his best to hide it from Chase.

"Yeah, Dad, just thinking about the trip," Chase said with a sigh.

"You nervous?" His dad put on the blinker and eased the truck off the highway.

"No. Why?" Chase realized he was white-knuckling the duffel bag, the red-faced Native American chief crumbling under his tight grip.

He loosened his grip and rubbed the logo until the folds eased out. "I'm just the youngest guy in the group."

His dad patted him on the shoulder. "It's because they like you and you're a hell of a football player. Just a sophomore and already the starting tight end for the varsity team. Oh, and they're predicting you to be All-State."

Chase shot his dad an inquisitive glance.

"Yes sir, read it in the paper this morning. I was going to wait till you got back, but it looked like you needed the pick me up."

A large, childish grin stretched across Chase's face. "All-State, huh?"

His dad nodded and turned another corner. They were traveling along a residential street now. Every house they passed was more expensive and luxurious than the one before it. There was old money here, and Chase's family clearly didn't belong. Some of these families, like Justin Jackson's, quarterback extraordinaire, made their money in politics. Some families owned logging companies, and some owned car dealerships. They were all wealthier than Chase's family could ever fathom.

They rounded the last turn and proceeded up a hill toward the white house at the top. It was the luxurious home of the town mayor, Jonathan Jackson. It sat by itself at the top of the hill and seemed to rise above the rest of the city. The driveway stretched up from the main road before circling around an extravagant marble fountain and snaking its way back to the road.

His dad slowed the truck to a stop. Through the windshield, they could see Justin loading duffel bags into the back of a white Jeep Wrangler. Justin, the stereotypical "Golden Boy," was a tall, blonde-haired, blue-eyed Adonis.

Trevor McKee was carrying large jugs of water down the front steps of the house. Trevor stood in stark contrast to the QB. The boy was a mountain of a man and very much the stereotypical redneck. When Chase discovered they were moving to Tall Oak, he looked up the football team. The school program said Trevor McKee was six foot six and three hundred and thirty pounds. When Chase met Trevor at the first summer practice, it was clear the program wasn't exaggerating; if anything, the program underestimated the giant's size. It was at that first practice he found out Trevor's friends called him Ford. The nickname didn't click at first, but one of the other linemen patted him on the back as he jogged past. "It's 'cause that sum'bitch is as big as a truck, man." He found out later the head coach of his new football team, Thomas McKee, was Ford's father. Everyone called him Coach Chevy, a fitting nickname for a man as large as his son.

His dad stopped the truck a few feet behind the white Jeep and shot his son an encouraging smile. "Have fun." His father held out his fist. Chase hesitated for a minute, maybe too long. Ford was staring at the truck now. His massive arms swung in a "come on" motion. Chase gave his dad a fist bump and climbed out of the truck. "Thanks, Dad."

"No problem, Mr. All-State."

His dad waved at Ford through the windshield as Chase slammed the truck door shut and proceeded up the remainder of the driveway to his teammate's Jeep. His heart sank a bit as the crunch of his dad's tires receded down the driveway. Despite being excited to go on the trip, he had this unexplainable angst building up inside.

When he was a few feet away, Ford clapped his hands and held them up like a catcher behind home plate. Chase tossed his duffel bag to him. The bag flew through the air, end over end. Ford caught the bag and, in one swift motion, tossed it into the back of the Jeep.

Justin turned around. The tall teen appeared even taller standing in the back of the open-top Jeep. He flashed a big smile. "The kid is here!" he shouted. Chase jokingly looked around and then pointed a finger at himself.

"I'm the kid?"

Justin jumped down from the back of the Jeep and held his hand out. Chase locked hands, and they half embraced.

"What's up, man? You ready for a kickass weekend?" Justin's boyish excitement forced a smile onto Chase's face. He could feel the nervousness dissipating from his body.

"Hell yeah, man!"

Justin turned toward Ford. "Hey man, in the garage is that big-ass bluetooth speaker. You think you can grab it?" Ford sighed and turned away from the Jeep, walking up the steps to the front door of the house. "Thanks, man! You know I'd get it myself, but. . ." Justin held up his hands. "I got soft baby hands." Ford held up his right hand and flashed the middle finger over his shoulder as he turned sideways and squeezed through the front door.

"Y'all been friends for a long time?" Chase asked.

Justin was already leaning over the back left tire, checking the pressure. Without looking up, he replied, "Since birth." He patted the tire and wiped his hands on his jeans, staining them with a streak of black grime. "Yeah, my pops was the QB at Tall Oak in the late eighties. Coach Chevy was his left tackle." He shrugged his shoulders. "Guess we're just keeping the tradition alive."

Chase loosed a little chuckle, relaxing a bit more.

"Guess you don't mind having the best tackle in the state watching your back. Anything I can do to help?"

Justin shook his head. "First off, he's the best tackle in the country, and nah man, we're about loaded up. We're just waiting for the rest of these fucktards to show up."

As if on cue, a horn blast ripped through the quiet morning air. The two turned to see a bright red F-150 ripping up the road toward the house at a high rate of speed. Post Malone's "Rockstar" blared from the speakers.

"Speak of the devil," Justin said.

As the truck pulled closer, they could see Irish's shiny red hair in the driver's seat. The truck squealed into the driveway before slamming to a stop. The red-headed boy leaned out the window, singing along with Post Malone about "fuckin' hoes" and feeling like a "rockstar." He shut off the truck and climbed out the window like a NASCAR driver. He pulled his duffel bag from the bed of the truck. The gold letters embroidered on the side read, "Cole 'Irish' Conners." He tossed the bag to Chase, who gently set it in the back of the Jeep. Irish ran up to Justin and jumped into his arms. Justin caught him, and Irish wrapped his legs around him, pretending to hump Justin's chest. He shouted, "We're about to have so much fucking fun!"

Justin pushed Irish off of him. "Get down, you soulless bastard." Irish hopped down.

"Bro, that episode of South Park came out like twenty years ago. When are you going to drop that lame-ass joke?"

Justin gripped the boy around the neck. "When your ginger ass convinces me you have one."

Irish bellowed an obnoxious laugh and turned to Chase.

"What's up, man? You ready to party?" Irish rammed his finger under his nose and made a sniffing sound.

Justin laughed at Chase's nervous expression, grabbing his shoulder. "Leave the kid alone, man."

Irish smacked Chase on the other shoulder. "I'm just fucking with you, buddy. We don't give coke to sophomores."

Justin shook his head. "You got everything you need?"

Irish nodded.

Another car was cruising up the hill toward the house. The chief's cruiser flipped on its red and blue lights and the siren roared to life, the sound reverberating off the house and through the boys' eardrums. Nick Sanders's deep voice erupted over the PA system. "You bitches ready to party?" The cruiser came to a stop behind Irish's blinged-out truck, and the siren went silent. The boys could see Chief Sanders wrestling the intercom away from his son as Lemichael, his other son, and Hector laughed hysterically in the back seat.

Justin swatted Chase on the arm and pointed at the car. "As I said," he muttered under his breath, "fucktards."

After a moment, Nick climbed out of the passenger seat and opened the rear passenger door to allow Lemichael and Hector out. Chief Sanders exited the cruiser with a groan. He rubbed at his knees before noticing Chase was watching him. "Tore my knees up playing ball with your coach back in the day."

The chief adjusted the utility belt that struggled to hold his bulging gut. The chief was a short man. His hairline had retreated to the point it was almost entirely invisible from the front. Chase had only seen him once before, but he could tell the man was athletic before age and fast food got to him. Thick thighs and muscular shoulders still rippled under his dark skin. Chase imagined the man would have been a nightmare to tackle forty years ago.

"Dad, can you pop the trunk?" Lemichael asked.

Chief Sanders leaned into the car and pulled a lever on the floorboard. The trunk popped open, and the three boys rummaged through it to get their bags. Hector and Lemichael began shoving each other and wrestling to get to their bags first. Nick stepped aside, waiting for the two boys. Chase had noticed early on that Nick was quieter than the others. Despite being twins, the only thing Lemichael and Nick had in common was their mutual love of football. Outside of that, Nick liked to read and got good grades. Lemichael was more of a class clown, always needing Nick's help to keep his grades up enough to play.

"Coach Chevy will shove his whole foot in my ass if you boys injure yourselves playing grab ass behind my car," Chief Sanders said. Hector shoved Lemichael a final time. The boys snatched their bags out of the back and walked over toward the Jeep. Chief Sanders rubbed the creases out of his khaki-colored uniform.

Behind Chase, Ford appeared in the doorway and, with a breathy wheeze, asked, "Any of you pussies want a shot?" Chase turned to see Ford's massive body blocking the front door. A large black speaker dangled from his left hand, and he held a bottle of Tito's Vodka above his head with the right. Chase watched the exasperated boy's flushed complexion drain when he saw the Chief of Police standing there.

Chief Sanders shook his head. "Y'all best wait till I'm long gone before starting any shenanigans."

The boys stood silently in their places. Chief Sanders smiled and winked at the boys before sliding back into his patrol car, rolling down the window as he slowly backed out of the driveway. He leaned out and shouted, "Y'all don't do anything too stupid, ya hear?"

Justin waved his hand. "Don't worry, Chief Sanders, I'll keep these boys in line."

The chief cracked a smile. "That's what I'm worried about." He sped off down the road, leaving them to their "shenanigans."

The boys busted out laughing. Hector cursed in Spanish. "Ford, you big cabrón, you couldn't have waited a few minutes?"

Ford was walking down the steps now. He tossed the speaker into the back of the Jeep, unscrewed the lid on the bottle, and took a massive swig. He loomed over Hector. "I gotta drink to deal with your Mexican ass," he said. Ford set the vodka into the back seat and clapped his hands again. The impact rippled across his beefy arms. "You bitches ready?"

Justin climbed into the back of the Jeep. "How many times are you going to call us bitches?" Justin asked. His spiked, blonde hair appeared almost white in the mid-morning sun.

"Wasn't talking to you, good buddy. I was talking to the Mexican and that soulless bastard over there," Ford said as he pointed at Irish. Irish smiled and waved a hand in the giant's direction. Justin bellowed a laugh.

Hector shot Ford the bird. "Fuck you, pendejo!"

Ford sneered at the smaller boy. "You know I don't speak that Mexican shit." The giant stared laser eyes into Hector before cracking a large smile.

Hector returned the grin. "And you know I can't stay mad at you, big boy."

Justin clapped his hands to get the boys' attention. "Alright, guys, before we go, I just want to say something. This is our last team trip together. All of us, except Hector and Chase, are seniors. After this season, Ford and I are going to Georgia, the Sanders twins are going to FAU, and Irish will probably go to jail." The boys busted out laughing.

Irish smacked Lemichael on the back. "Tell your pops to go easy on me, alright?"

"Seriously though," Justin continued, "y'all have been the best guys a QB and team captain could ask for. So, since this is the last of our annual team trips, I propose that it be the best one." The boys erupted into a chorus of cheers. "I expect each of you bitches to party your ass off. We'll make enough memories on this trip to last a lifetime!"

"And I'll drink enough to forget all those memories," Irish shouted.

Justin dove off the back of the Jeep toward Ford, who stuck out his massive bear paws and snagged Justin midair. He held him up like in the scene from *Dirty Dancing*. The boys erupted into a series of cheers again as Justin stuck his hands out from his side. Chase couldn't help but marvel at the ridiculous scene. Ford lowered Justin back to the ground, and the QB spun his finger around over his head.

"Load up!"

Chase hesitated when he realized there weren't enough seats. Justin slid into the driver's seat, Ford into the passenger. Hector, Nick, and Lemichael piled into the rear seats. Irish climbed into the back of the Jeep and reclined over the duffel bags and equipment. He patted at the duffel bag next to him. "Don't worry, you beautiful man. They can't see us back here." Chase shook his head and climbed into the Jeep. He reclined across the rest of the luggage, head on the opposite side of Irish.

The engine roared to life. The boys waited while Justin's phone connected to the Jeep's Bluetooth. "Party and Bullshit" by Biggie Smalls blasted through the speakers. Peeking over the rear seats, Chase saw Justin slide on some Oakleys and smack the dashboard. The Jeep's tires spun slightly as it lurched forward.

Chapter 2

Tiffany Thomas sat beside her dad, Austin Thomas, in a small square room. Cheap paint peeled off the decaying bricks that made up the walls, exposing the brick's original dark gray color. She and her father sat in metal folding chairs, the cold of which permeated through her thin clothing and up her back, leaving a trail of goosebumps. She attempted to pull the chair closer to the table only to discover the chair had been bolted to the ground. There was a small window on the wall to her left, maybe a foot tall and a couple of feet wide. A white, rubbery substance coated the window, blocking out nearly all the warmth and light. Outside, it was the beginning of summer, a typical June in Florida. Just like every other day that month, it was a scorching ninety-five degrees, one hundred percent humidity, and a heat index of one hundred and ten. Inside the police station it might as well have been the North Pole. Frigid air poured from the air vent in the ceiling. Every few minutes, the air conditioning would stutter and a blast of cold air would swoosh through the room. She wondered if they kept it this cold to make the criminals feel uncomfortable while being interrogated, and suddenly, she felt like a criminal.

She wanted to get up and leave. They could tell Officer Lopez it had all been a mistake, some major misunderstanding. Maybe it could all be a bad dream. They could just move on and forget about the whole ordeal. She wanted to pretend it never happened.

Her dad placed a comforting hand on her back, and Tiffany involuntarily shuddered at his touch. He withdrew his hand and placed it back in his own lap. A pang of guilt ripped through her as she stared down at the hands that used to comfort her. He rubbed his fingers together, reddening his right thumb. This was his stress indicator. Her father had done it for as long as she could remember. Austin Thomas was the kindest man and a gentle father. He worked as a lawn care guy for the rich people on the other side of town. She knew her father didn't have much money, but she and her sister were never made to want for anything. His only rule was they all attended mass together once a week. He was a devout man and a well-known member of the only Catholic Church in town, often attending events with Father White and volunteering his time helping the homeless at shelters in Tallahassee.

Tiffany scanned the room for a clock and realized nothing adorned the walls. This must be another interrogation tactic the police used, similar to casinos. Her grandfather had been a big gambler, and one time when he failed to pick her up from school, her father explained a man could lose all sense of time in a casino.

Tiffany wiggled in her seat, eyeing the blue door that led to the rest of the police station. She wondered again if her father would let her leave. She didn't wonder long; he was bullheaded and firmly believed in justice. Austin Thomas once gave a guest lecture at the church, after a hurricane, about how the rule of law and their devout belief in God held the community together. She loved her father, but his naivety worried her. This was a small town, and her assailant was best friends with both the chief's kid and the mayor's kid.

Despite the frigid air, her hands began to sweat. She pulled her knees to her chin. Trying to warm herself up and hide her shame, she wrapped her arms around them and sunk her face down behind her knees.

Her father reached out toward her again, but he stopped short. His hand lingered between them for a moment. He left it suspended in the air before pulling it back to his lap.

Tears welled up in her eyes. A single tear rolled down her cheek and hung off her chin. The air licked at the moisture on her face.

Her heart dropped into her stomach as she heard two hard knocks on the door. Her stomach twisted itself into a knot as Officer Lopez entered the room. He wore a khaki-colored uniform. A brown folder was tucked beneath one arm, and a white styrofoam cup full of what Tiffany presumed to be coffee was in his other hand. He moved his arm and allowed the folder to fall onto the table. He took a loud, obnoxious sip, accented with a smacking of his lips. He set the cup down and took the chair across from Tiffany and her dad. Tiffany couldn't help but notice his relaxed posture. The officer slouched against the back of the chair, and the top couple buttons of his uniform were undone, exposing what had once been a white undershirt but was now stained yellow from sweat. She gawked at the unprofessional appearance of the man representing the town police department.

"Mr. Thomas, what brings you in here today?" Officer Lopez flipped open the folder and removed a notebook. The officer retrieved a pen from the breast pocket of his uniform, clicked it three times, and pressed it against the paper. He spun the pen in small circles until the blue ink coated a small corner of the paper.

"My, uh, my daughter was. . ." He paused and gulped. It sounded like he was choking on the word. "Assaulted."

Officer Lopez glanced up from his paper. "Do you think you can elaborate?"

Her father glanced down. She watched his lips moving in silent prayer. He rubbed furiously at his fingers.

"I was raped."

The steadiness of her own voice surprised her. She raised her head momentarily from behind her knees and returned it to its hiding place as soon as the words left her mouth. Her father whispered something about God.

Officer Lopez jotted a note in his notebook. Tiffany could see Officer Lopez had written "RAPED" in all capital letters. He studied the girl, his dark eyes scanning her for something, Tiffany couldn't be sure, but it looked like he was trying to determine if she was lying.

"I'm sorry that happened to you. Do you know who it was?"

Tiffany didn't raise her head. She was afraid of this part. This was the part where her father found out who violated her. Soon, the entire town would call her a liar. This was the part when the whole town would take the side of the woman-abusing asshole. She knew they were going to call her a whore, murmuring about how she must have gotten drunk and then regretted it. Nobody would believe her, and it was all because her rapist was Coach Chevy's son.

"Ford," Tiffany muttered under her breath.

Officer Lopez leaned in. "I'm sorry, I couldn't quite hear you."

The tears spilled down Tiffany's face now. They fished out of her ducts and punched a path down her cheeks. She wiped the tears away, only for them to be replaced with more.

"Ford," her voice cracked. She could feel sobs welling up inside her. They were swirling around in her chest, mixing with the sudden urge to vomit at the mention of her assailant's name. She began shaking uncontrollably.

Officer Lopez stopped writing. The three of them sat in a prolonged silence.

"Ford? You mean Trevor McKee?"

She wiped the tears away again and nodded.

"Coach Chevy's kid raped you? Is that what you're telling me?" His voice carried no empathy. The officer's accusatory tone replaced the bored one he had begun the conversation with. Tiffany was taken aback. She stared at the officer in front of her, mouth open.

Her dad chimed in. "Sir, why aren't you writing any of this down?"

Officer Lopez didn't bother addressing Mr. Thomas. He stared at Tiffany, a wild look in his eye. "Now Tiffany, I need you to understand what you're accusing Ford of."

Tiffany's feet slid off her chair. She slammed fists into the table between them. "No! I need you to understand what I am saying happened." She slipped her hands back into her lap. Pain radiated up her arms.

The officer reclined in his chair and scribbled a few notes in his notebook. "Ok then," he said. "Tell me everything."

Tiffany glanced at her father, whose head hung in shame. He stared intently at the tiles of the floor. Her face reddened. She knew she was blameless, but the sudden rush of shame threatened to shut her entire body down. Would her father still love her after she told this story? Would she still be his little girl? She sniffed in, sucking in the mucus running from her nose.

"Well, Ford and I. . ." She swallowed the bile pooling in the back of her throat. She hated that her body was having physical reactions to his name. "We've been hanging out after school." She could feel her father's gaze on her now. Tiffany knew she wasn't allowed to be alone with boys. She could feel the sense of betrayal radiating off her father. "I thought he liked me." The tears flowed again. "And, uh, we were making out in his room." Her father's stare burned into the side of her head like laser beams. "He tried to take it further and I said I wasn't ready."

Officer Lopez leaned in. "And?"

"And that's when he raped me." The confidence she exuded when proclaiming it the first time had faded. Her voice came out shaken, and her bottom lip trembled.

"Did he hit you or anything?"

"No, but he was very aggressive. He tore my shirt and broke the clasp on my bra."

The officer nodded and jotted down a few more notes. "Did you fight back?" His accusatory tone returned.

"I couldn't."

"Why not?"

"He's really strong, and I was scared."

"Did you tell him to stop?"

"I begged him to."

"And what did he say?"

Tiffany pulled back into her seat. She returned her knees to their defensive position and buried her head. She mumbled a response.

Officer Lopez leaned in even closer, stretched about halfway over the table. His pen lay idly on his open notepad.

"He called me a cock tease!"

The officer recoiled at her outburst. He composed himself and picked up the pen, writing down the last of his notes. "If y'all will excuse me, I'm going to grab the chief." He got up and disappeared through the large blue door that separated them from the rest of the world.

Her father rubbed his fingers vigorously. The skin on his left thumb turned a deep shade of pink.

The door swung open a moment later and Chief Sanders leaned in. "Mr. Thomas, can I speak to you out here for a minute?"

Tiffany watched her father stop rubbing his fingers. Without a verbal response, he stood up and exited the room. Tiffany rocked subtly in the chair and squeezed her knees tightly to her chest. The sudden emptiness of the room was overwhelming. Her heart rate sped up and her breathing became labored. The room made her feel small and weak. She waited for what felt like an hour for her father and the chief to return to the room. Her father entered first, followed by Officer Lopez and Chief Sanders.

Her father didn't return to his seat. He leaned against the wall next to the door. His body faced Tiffany, but his head hung toward the ground.

Chief Sanders picked up the notepad Officer Lopez had been writing on and skimmed the notes. Tiffany watched as his eyes darted across the page and back to the start of the next line. The chief tossed the pad onto the table, then walked around the table and stood next to Tiffany. He sat on the table, one leg remaining on the floor. "So, what I understand is that you are accusing Ford McKee of raping you, is that right?"

Tiffany was shaking now. The chief's menacing presence loomed over her. His shadow cast across her face. She nodded.

"But you were in his bed and making out with him willingly?"

She tried to swallow the lump growing in her throat. She nodded.

"Well, Tiffany, let me tell you how I see it. I see a girl who was probably star-struck by Ford McKee. You probably know that boy will be in the NFL someday. I think y'all had a breakdown in communication."

"No, that's-"

"Don't interrupt me, girl. I don't think you made your protests known. You probably never told him no. I think you slept with Ford McKee, regretted it, and tried to find a way to alleviate yourself of the guilt of having sex outside of marriage. Does that sound right?"

Heat flooded Tiffany's ears. "No! That's not what happened! Dad?" She looked in her dad's direction.

He shook his head. "Come on, sweetie, let's go home."

The chief jumped up from the table. He picked up the pad of paper and ripped it into tiny shreds, dropping the little pieces into a small trash can previously obscured from Tiffany's view. "Yup, I think you oughta listen to your father."

Tiffany balked. She felt glued to her chair. She felt the firm grip of her father's hand on her arm. He half held her up and half dragged her out of the station, pulling her past hundreds of accusatory eyes. The world spun around her as she struggled to catch her breath. The realization of what happened slowly sank in. The nausea Tiffany had been experiencing since her harrowing attack made its vicious return, and she heaved into the bushes outside the police station. Her father held her hair back to avoid getting any vomit in it. When she finished, she wiped her mouth on her sleeve and peered through the glass doors of the police station. Standing near the interrogation room, she could see Chief Sanders and Officer Lopez laughing. The weight of her body became too much for her knees, and they buckled under her weight. She slumped into her father's arms. He slid her into the passenger seat of his truck. Through her window, she could see the entrance of the police station. The gold lettering below the city logo read, "Justice for all."

Chapter 3

"Shots!"

Someone had yelled it from the kitchen. The rest of his teammates were already in there. Chase was hiding in the living room, trying to guzzle as much water as he could stomach. However, the more water he drank, the drunker he became.

Irish poked his head around the corner, his red hair flowing wildly with the motion. He threw his hands up to either side. "Don't be a pussy," he jeered.

Just like the last five times, Chase pushed himself out of the La-Z-Boy recliner. His legs wobbled beneath him as his equilibrium failed. The room shifted around, giving the impression the room was spinning. This would be the last shot, he lied to himself. His hand left the armrest of the recliner, and he half walked, half fell into the wall separating the kitchen and living room. The wall felt cool against his shirtless shoulders. He elected to slide along it instead of attempting to stand upright. He negotiated the wall and wrapped himself around the door frame. Grasping the counter, he managed to right himself and tried to play it cool.

Ford was standing in the back of the kitchen holding a bottle of vodka. Those massive meat hooks he called hands made the handle look tiny. Chase could have sworn they opened that bottle a few minutes ago, but it was already over half empty. His eyes floated down to the table, where a collection of two empty vodka bottles sat upon a throne of crushed beer cans. The behemoth of a man took a massive swig directly from the container. He returned it to his side and exhaled like he was breathing fire. "I said shots, you pussies!" The words came out in a slurred mess, sounding more like Ford had a speech impediment than an alcohol problem.

"Where's Lemichael?" Hector asked.

As if summoned into existence, Lemichael came strutting into the room wearing only his boxers. The boys stared at him.

"Dude, what the fuck?" Justin asked through a laugh.

"It's hot as a motherfucker in here."

Everyone burst out laughing. Lemichael followed that statement up with, "I don't know how I got talked into going into the woods with a bunch of rednecks."

"We prefer the term Appalachian Americans," Ford barked.

"I don't give a fuck."

Ford cocked his free hand back and pretended to swing at Lemichael. Justin jumped between them, arms raised in surrender. Behind him, Lemichael took a goofy boxing stance and bobbed his head around in his best Muhammed Ali impression.

"Everybody chill. We're all going to take a shot, smoke some weed, and then I have a very special treat for you," Justin said.

Ford grunted his agreement and poured his bottle of vodka across the seven shot glasses on the counter. The aroma wafted across the room and assaulted Chase's nose. His eyes watered, and his gut wrenched at the thought of the coming shot. He wasn't sure how much more he could take. Being only fifteen, he was three years younger than the rest of the guys. Hell, this was his first time getting drunk. He had downed a few beers here and there, but nothing like the back-to-back shots they were putting down.

Justin passed the shots out to each person. Without waiting for the others, Irish tilted his head back and drained the shot glass. Justin shot him a dirty look.

"Oops, spilled it," Irish said as he held up the empty shot glass.

"Yeah, down your throat, you fucking alcoholic," Nick chided. Irish smirked as Ford poured him another shot.

Chase's world started spinning, and Justin's face seemed blurry. Chase couldn't tell if it was from the tears forming in his eyes or the spinning sensation overtaking him. He leaned back against the wooden walls of the cabin and squeezed his eyes shut. He silently tried to force the world to stop spinning.

He could hear Irish yell, "We're losing him!" Irish's taunts seemed to be filtered through water, both challenging to decipher and incredibly muffled.

One of the other boys yelled, "He's gonna puke!"

As soon as the word "puke" hit his eardrums, the burning sensation of bile sprinted up from his stomach. He pushed past the other boys, knocking Irish over on the way. He leaned over the empty sink and heaved.

The team cheered!

Someone yelled, "First one down!"

From his position on the ground, Irish yelled, "Puke and rally!"

In unison, the boys started chanting, "Puke and rally." The chant was slow at first. It gradually grew faster until the boys could barely get the words out. Chase turned on the faucet, flushing cold water through his mouth and swishing it between his teeth. The water was refreshing to his dehydrated mouth. He spit the water back into the sink. Gathering his resolve, he turned to face the guys.

They were in a frenzy now. The chants of "puke and rally" were no longer in unison. They bellowed and whooped like wild animals all around him. A frenzy of jumping and wrestling unfolded before him. Justin stepped forward and handed Chase a fresh shot glass, spilling over the poisonous liquid. He sucked in a deep breath. Justin pushed the shot glass into his hand and gripped his fist. Justin ushered Chase's hands toward his mouth and forced Chase to put the shot glass to his lips. Chase complied. He tilted his head back and swallowed. His gag reflex kicked in as the warm liquid worked its way down his throat, and for a moment, he thought he would throw up again, but he managed to stifle the urge.

The boys went wild. They jumped around and patted him on the shoulders and back. Ford even picked him up and lifted him high enough to touch the vaulted ceiling of the cabin. The evening turned into a drunken blur of debauchery after that. They turned the place upside down. Nick cranked the radio to its highest setting, the adrenaline-inducing sound of "Sabotage" by The Beastie Boys reverberating off the walls. They jumped from the couches. Justin rode on Ford's back. They threw a football around, breaking several light fixtures in the process.

Chase collapsed into the brown La-Z-Boy. The poor chair moaned under his weight. It had been several hours since he puked and rallied, and the room was spinning again. Justin sneaked water bottles to Chase throughout the night, a gesture Chase was incredibly grateful for at that moment. He had spent much of the night in a drunken supor, flirting with blacking out. The constant water bottles Justin supplied were probably the only reason he hadn't succumbed to the copious amounts of liquor.

One by one, the boys collapsed onto the various bits of furniture in the living room. Ford took up the entirety of a brown loveseat, Nick, Lemichael, and Hector on the sofa, and Irish stretched across the floor. Justin stood in front of them, to the left of the large flat-screen TV mounted on the wall above a fireplace made of stones.

A wicked-looking grin stretched across his face. "Alright, boys, here is the moment we've all been waiting for." All the boys except Chase cheered. He wasn't sure what Justin was talking about, but everyone's excitement was contagious. To his left, Lemichael produced a joint. Sparking it up, the poignant stench of marijuana permeated the cabin.

Taking the blunt, Justin flicked on the TV. He ran an HDMI cable from a Mac laptop to the TV. His laptop screen appeared on the TV screen, revealing the team's logo, his jersey number under it, and various icons spread across the home screen in an unorganized fashion. He took one more puff and passed it to Chase.

Chase held the joint between his thumb and pointer finger. He rolled it around and examined it.

"It's alright, man, the shit will be out of your system within thirty days, and the state can't drug test us for another forty-five. We have you covered," Justin encouraged.

"This is the only time you can do it, though. If you get us in trouble during the season, I will fuck you up," Nick said.

Chase simply nodded and pressed the joint to his lips, inhaling deeply. The burning sensation rushed down his throat and expanded in his lungs. He quickly exhaled and fell into a coughing fit. The other guys laughed.

Hector leaned forward. "Let me take that from you, Willie Nelson." The other boys erupted into an even bigger laughing session. Chase tried to laugh between bouts of coughing.

Justin pressed play again. The video showed the two of them on the bed making out. They pulled off each other's clothes. His girlfriend's breasts faced the camera when she shifted her weight to remove her pants. Chase hung his head; unable to bring himself to watch, he rubbed his hands through the back of his hair. He thought about leaping up and smashing the laptop, but Ford never sat down after their confrontation. The giant lingered, just far enough out of the way so everyone could see the TV but not far enough that Chase could do anything without being intercepted.

The video played on, but Chase refused to look up. His teammates watched it silently, a stark contrast to their previous reactions. Their lack of response only made Chase more uncomfortable. The sounds of sexual panting echoed through the otherwise silent cabin. Chase felt like the video would never end. He could hear himself gasp on the video, and it was over. Sitting in that room, the other boys watching a sex tape he didn't know he made, was the longest three minutes of his life.

Hector strutted across the room and patted him on the back. "You did good, kid."

The others burst out laughing. "What the fuck was that?" Lemichael asked.

"You did good, kid," Justin mocked in an old man's voice.

Chase couldn't respond; he was overcome with emotions as a mix of shame and anger flooded over him. The desire to fight everyone in the room built up inside him. Justin walked across the room, knelt down in front of Chase, and placed a hand on the back of his head. "There's a price to pay to be in this brotherhood. We've all paid it. It keeps us safe." He leaned his head against the top of Chase's head. "You're one of us now."

The other boys jumped around and cheered. Chase tried to stifle a smile. Despite the anger, being part of the group felt good. A spike of guilt drove through his heart, but he shook it off and looked up at Justin.

"I'll delete it after the trip ends," Justin promised. Reluctantly, Chase nodded.

Justin leaped to his feet and clapped his hands. "Alright, you horny assholes, we got a big day tomorrow. It is," Justin paused to look at his watch, one hand over his eyes and squinting at the little hands, "two a.m. Everyone better get some sleep. I have an action-packed day planned for us."

Justin turned off the TV and faced his teammates. "Oh, and after our special little gift, I think it's only fair that Chase gets the guest bedroom."

Ford grunted his displeasure at the proclamation but returned to his position on the loveseat.

The other boys began shuffling around, zombified in their inebriated state. Chase still hadn't worked up the strength to stand. He watched as Justin walked toward the master bedroom; he held the door partially closed and winked at Chase before shutting it all the way.

You can.

With that, she raised the camera and snapped a picture of herself in the mirror. The towel covered her from the waist down, but the camera focused on her bare breasts. The mirror was still steamy from the shower. She paused for a moment, swallowed hard, and pressed send.

Her father's voice snapped her back to the present. "So tell me again how the picture got out." His voice seemed more understanding this time.

A tear rolled down her face as Hector's betrayal tore into her core.

"I don't know, Daddy. I sent the picture to Hector."

Her dad stopped pacing.

"Hector Lopez?"

"Yes."

More tears worked their way down her cheeks, clinging to her jawline before dropping freely onto her lap.

"Why would you send a picture like that?" Just like that, the anger returned.

She wiped the tears away from her cheeks. A warm feeling rushed up from her toes and radiated throughout her body. She expected her answer to sound pitiful. The anger in it surprised her.

"I thought he loved me."

Her mother let out an audible sob. She was only in her mid forties, but poor health had aged her prematurely. She stuck her frail hands out, and Natalie took them into her own. Her mother rubbed her thumbs along the back of Natalie's hands. She expected the act to soothe her, but it made her feel like a child. The look in her mother's eyes was one of pity, causing a rush of anger to boil up inside of Natalie.

"So Hector sent the photo to everyone?"

"He said he didn't. Someone took his phone."

Her father walked to the end of the kitchen table and dropped himself into the seat. The squeak of the legs on the tile sent a shiver down her spine. George fished the pack of smokes from his pocket and sparked another. Natalie's mother opened her mouth to protest, but thought better of it.

"Did he say who took his phone?"

Natalie shook her head. The tears weren't flowing anymore, replaced with dry salt lines.

"It must have been one of the guys on the football team. They probably took it out of his locker or something. A bunch of my friends got the text." She fought the urge to cry again, marveling at how many tears she could produce in a single day. "They didn't know the number. One of my guy friends mentioned something about burner phones. He said nobody can trace them back to anyone."

She pulled her hands away from her mother, conscious of the hurt expression stretched across her mother's face but unable to stifle the need to clench her fists. She wanted to punch something. She wanted to punch herself for trusting a boy, wanted to punch Hector, wanted to punch whoever stole his phone and sent the photo out.

Her father reclined in his seat. "Hector's dad is a police officer," he said. "I suppose I should go talk to the chief tomorrow."

Natalie shook her head. "It won't do any good."

Her father leaned forward. He planted his elbows firmly on the table and sucked in a lungful of smoke. He exhaled slowly. "What else can we do, Nat?"

Her mother interjected. "I'm not sure, George, but we both know the chief won't help

us here."

not nearly as thick. For a moment, Nick thought he might still be dreaming because the man who wore the costume was the thing of nightmares. The entire scene caused the cramping sensation to return to his bladder.

The man cocked his head slightly to the right, and the rabbit's face locked on his. The man lifted a hand and waved. It wasn't a wave you give your neighbor, or a swift motion with the hand. This wave felt menacing. The palm faced Nick, and the masked man wiggled his fingers.

Nick's mouth hung ajar. A scream lodged itself in his throat and refused to release.

The man in the rabbit mask walked backward. He slowly faded from the light and into the crushing darkness of the forest.

The weight holding him down and silencing his scream lifted as the masked man disappeared from his view. He waited for his senses to slowly return before turning away from the window.

"Guuuuyyyysss!" His cry was a cross between a whine and a scream. He fled the bathroom, his bare feet smacking the wooden floor with meaty thuds. He rushed down the hallway to where his teammates slept. "Guys, guys, guys," he shouted as he ran.

Sprinting around the hallway's corner, his feet kicked a large, soft object on the floor. The impact sent him tumbling into the coffee table at the center of the room. The large object he kicked groaned and rolled over.

"Nick, what the fuck, man?"

Somewhere in the room, Nick heard the flick of a switch. Light flooded the room, and his teammates' displeased groans greeted it. Justin was standing near the front door, his hand still resting on the light switch.

The large, soft thing he had tripped over was Lemichael. He must have passed out on the floor near the couch.

"Nick, what the fuck are you doing?" Justin's face was a mix of exhaustion and anger.

Nick's breath wouldn't return. His chest heaved up and down despite only running a few feet. He raised a shaky hand toward the bathroom. He tried to speak, but the weight he felt in his throat when he saw the man in the rabbit mask had returned. His speech came out in slurred half-words. "Th- there. M-m-man."

"There's a man?" Justin asked incredulously.

Nick looked to see Irish sitting straight up on the couch now. His red hair was messy, and his eyes blinked rapidly in the harsh lighting. His friends stared at him with confused looks.

Nick shook his head. He tried to force the words out, but they hooked themselves in his throat.

"Go check that shit out," Justin said to Irish.

Irish let out a groan but didn't protest beyond that. He pushed himself up, his legs wobbling momentarily. The booze and drowsiness were clearly taking a toll on him. He shambled down the hallway like a drunken zombie.

Nick crawled on his hands and knees past Lemichael. Lemichael punched him in the shoulder as he did, but the punch didn't even register in Nick's mind. His eyes fixated on the back of Irish's head. The light from the living room reached farther into the hall than the LED clock. He could see all the way down the hall and into the still-illuminated bathroom.

He watched as Irish entered the bathroom and looked out the window. His messy red hair fell wildly as he made a show of looking in all directions. He shook his head and yelled, "Maybe in here!" His arm hit the shower curtain and flung it open. The rings holding it up screamed as they scraped down the rod.

He looked back at Nick. "Room's empty, bro."

He flicked off the light and walked back into the living room. Irish stepped directly on Lemichael. "Oops, didn't see you there," he laughed. Lemichael took a lazy kick at Irish's heels, and Irish slumped back into his spot on the couch.

"Justin, turn the light out," Ford grumbled.

"Hang on a second." Justin glared at Nick, "You good?"

Nick shook his head. His breathing slowed, and he felt confident his speaking ability was returning.

"There was a guy in a rabbit mask."

Irish sat back up.

Justin shook his head. "What?"

"A fucking rabbit mask, man. Like a plastic Halloween mask. You put the shit on your face and a little string around the back of your head."

The rest of the boys sat up, except for Ford. Ford lay on the loveseat, cradling an empty bottle of vodka and shielding his eyes with one enormous hand.

Justin's face remained neutral as he continued to stare at Nick.

"It was a fucking man in a rabbit mask. He stepped out of the trees. He waved at me and then walked backward into the trees. A fucking man."

Nick felt the perspiration running down his neck. His friends stared at him as if he had three heads. Rage built up at their lack of response.

"Ain't no man," Ford stated.

"I saw him," Nick insisted.

"It was probably just a dream," Chase offered.

Chase had been sleeping in the bedroom opposite the master. Justin encouraged him to take the bed after the whole video incident. Nick would have thought Justin felt bad for his little voyeurism show if Justin had ever shown remorse before. Nick knew better though. He had encouraged the kid to take a bed to earn some goodwill. It was the same kind of thing he did to Nick all those years ago.

Nick shook his head. "Nah, man."

The boys sat silently, looking about the room at each other. None of them seemed to know what to do next. Justin finally broke the stalemate by flicking off the light.

"Everyone get some sleep. We're miles from town. There's nobody out there."

No sooner had the words left his mouth when the Jeep's car alarm ripped through the night air. The Jeep's flashing lights illuminated the living room, washing everything in an eerie yellow hue. The light quickly retreated, only to return again.

Nick could see Justin's face in that split second when the yellow light flooded through the window. He could see the fear in Justin's eyes, and Nick's heart froze. Justin was never afraid. He was the model of confidence and poise in the face of danger. The yellow light retreated. It came back, along with the incessant beeping of the car's alarm. In that brief instant, the look had flushed away. Justin had composed himself and flipped on the light.

All the boys, except Justin, jumped to their feet and rushed to the window, jockeying for position. Their faces pressed against the cool glass, and they scanned the area in front of the cabin for any sign of life. The Jeep continued flashing its lights and screaming out.

The boys couldn't see the Jeep from the window. It was too far to the left, closer to the front door. Suddenly, the Jeep stopped screaming and instead released two innocent beeps. Nick recognized the beeps as the sound of the Jeep being unlocked. He looked over his shoulders to see Justin holding the key fob in his hand.

"What was that?" Lemichael asked. His words came out breathless.

"Probably an animal climbing on the Jeep." Justin tossed the key fob back onto the table by the front door.

"Or a man in a rabbit mask," Hector joked as he punched Nick's arm.

"I'll go check it out." Ford pushed away from the window and lumbered around the couch. His massive body caused the wooden floors to bend and moan.

"It can wait till morning," Justin reassured him.

Ford shook his head. "If I don't go look," he pointed at the other boys still huddled around the window, "they'll be pissing themselves all night."

Justin nodded and stepped aside. Ford slid the deadbolt from its locked position and tossed the door open. He canted himself at a forty-five-degree angle and scooted through the open doorway. Nick watched through the window as the giant appeared on the front porch. Ford stood there for a moment and gazed out over the tree line. He reached back through the open front door and flicked on the porch lights, which painted the grassy patch between the porch and trees in light.

Ford paused after he stepped off the porch. His head swiveled slowly from side to side. Nick could see the profile of his fat face. The one eye Nick could see squinted against the darkness. Ford turned his torso back toward the window and stuck up his fat middle finger. A few of the boys chuckled. Nick ignored the obscene gesture and watched the tree line intently.

Ford turned toward the direction of the Jeep and took a few steps before freezing. He jerked his head back in the direction of the tree line. Nick's heart thumped against the walls of his chest. One boy whispered, "What is he. . ." but the last word trailed into oblivion.

Ford stepped toward the tree line and shouted, "If someone is out there, I will fuck you up." To punctuate his threat, he smacked his hands together. The loud clap reverberated through the woods. He took another step; he was only a few feet from the tree line now.

Nick wished Ford would come back. He willed his friend to turn around. They could lock the door and wait for morning. The image of the masked man burned itself into his mind.

In unison, three figures stepped out from behind the trees. All three men wore the same blue jumpsuit and plastic rabbit masks. They stood just inside the tree line, partially obscured in darkness. The light from the porch glinted off of a shiny object in the rightmost man's hand. From his vantage point, Nick couldn't tell what it was.

Ford took one step away from the three men. They matched his movement, each taking a step forward, the precision of their movements sending goosebumps running down Nick's back.

"What the—"

Justin cut off Ford before he could finish. "Ford, lookout!" Justin's frantic voice called from the open door.

Ford jerked to the left. He lifted his massive left arm to shield himself from a fourth man. The man swung something at Ford. Even from within the cabin, Nick could hear the sound of something hard striking his friend. The deafening crack of metal on bone turned his stomach.

A splash of liquid sprayed across the ground. It reached as far as the end of the front porch, staining the wooden floorboards a bright red.

Ford fell backward, away from his attacker, and collapsed to the ground. His screams echoed through the forest and bounced around the cabin's walls. None of the boys moved. None of them screamed. Nick wasn't even sure they were breathing.

Moving as one, the three men standing by the tree line came forward. Ford scooted himself away from them, his wide frame carving a path in the dirt as he crawled toward the cabin. He gripped his left arm with his right. Blood seeped through his fingers and decorated the grass. They surrounded Ford, the shiny objects now in clear view. The four men held machetes.

What happened next played out in slow motion, like a scene from a movie. Nick's mind seemed too slow to process what it was seeing. The four men lifted their machetes over their heads, holding them high in the air. The light of the moon reflected harshly off their blades.

Ford begged for his life. He pleaded and tried to make deals. A series of incomprehensible sentences left the giant's mouth as he squirmed away from his assailants.

One man nodded, and the four men brought down their blades. In a savage dance, they took turns smashing their blades down on Ford, their machetes biting into his skin. Blood squirted from Ford's open wounds and flew wildly through the air each time one of the rabbits removed their blade from his pulverized body. The fingers from his right hand went flying toward the cabin with one swing. His left hand collapsed to the ground with another. The blades cut deep. They exposed tendons. Bones jutted in every direction. For one fleeting moment, Nick locked eyes with Ford. Nick knew that if he survived the night, the desperation in Ford's eyes would scar him for life. One of the men brought their machete down and severed Ford's nose and cheek.

The macabre display continued for what felt like an hour. The men hacked away at the boy beneath them. For a while, Ford fought back. He even tried to stand up once. One of the masked men put that to an end by running his blade through Ford's Achilles tendon. Ultimately, Ford curled into the fetal position and cried for his mother as the men ruthlessly hacked at him.

The boys stared through the open window. Eventually, one of the men quit swinging his machete. Another followed his lead. Finally, the other two stopped swinging. The assailant's machetes hung limply at their sides. Their chests heaved up and down; Nick could hear their panting through the thick panel of the window.

One of the men turned his head toward the window. His rabbit mask was soaked in Ford's blood, and bits of flesh clung to the ears. The man's blue jumpsuit was nearly black with blood and gore.

The four men turned away from the cabin, retreating to the tree line in lockstep. Three of them continued into the darkness and disappeared from sight as the fourth man turned back toward the group. He held up his hand and wiggled his four fingers. Nick's blood ran cold as he watched the man turn away and walk into the darkness of the forest.

Chapter 6

Imani Winston adjusted her tight-feeling shirt as she stared at the clock hanging on the wall. She sank deeper into her chair as the second hand ticked away.

Principal Debra Walsh sat across from Imani. The small woman appeared even smaller behind her enormous desk. Imani thought about how the older kids made fun of their principal for overcompensating her petite stature with such a monstrosity of a desk. Now she understood why.

Principal Walsh's beady eyes flicked up to the clock and then back to the paper on her desk. She tapped a gold pen against the desk.

Imani looked back at the clock, anxiously waiting for the door to open and for her father to arrive. She turned back around and fixated on Principal Walsh's pen; it smacked off pace with the second hand.

Tick. Smack. Tick. Smack.

The two sat in near silence. Only the smacking of the pen made any noticeable noise. She wondered if she should say something to break the stalemate, maybe explain to the principal why she had requested this meeting. She also contemplated getting up and leaving the office. Imani continued examining the enormous desk and checking the clock, which made her feel small and weak.

Three eighteen.

There was a soft knock on the office door. It cracked open, and Principal Walsh's assistant stuck her head in. The woman's brown hair was slowly coming undone from the bun on her head. Imani thought she looked flustered. She would be, too, if she had to report to Principal Walsh all day.

"Principal Walsh, Mr. Winston is here for your meeting."

Principal Walsh didn't respond. She just waved one of her skeleton hands toward the woman. The assistant entered the room and held the door for Imani's father.

He entered the room, holding his blue work hat in his hands. He nodded at the assistant as he passed. "Thank you, ma'am."

The assistant smiled and closed the door behind her as she left. Imani's father pulled the collar of his jumpsuit down, revealing the dirt and grime that coated his dark skin. It looked out of place in this pristine office, but she supposed he had done it to look more professional.

Soot from the factory stained his steel-toed work boots. Her father had been so proud when her mother surprised him with them one Christmas morning. He beamed as he told her it was the first new pair of boots he had ever owned. Of course, that was before her mother died. It was the last Christmas they spent together as a family, and he had been wearing the same worn-out pair of boots every day since.

Her eyes flicked back to Principal Walsh in time to see her grimace as she stared at the black footprints her father had left in his wake.

Imani wasn't sure exactly what he did. All she knew was her father left before she got up for school and came home every day exhausted and dirty.

He brushed his hands on his pants and outstretched his hand. "Mikeis Winston, pleasure to meet you." His gruff voice sounded strange in this room. It was almost too deep to travel around the massive furniture of the principal's office. Her mother used to attend parent-teacher conferences and meet with school staff; mother once told her it was because her father tended to be rather direct. Knowing this put Imani on edge. She was afraid he might say the wrong thing and was afraid this meeting could make the situation even worse.

Principal Walsh jammed her bony fingers into Mr. Winston's hand awkwardly. "Principal Walsh," she introduced herself. She wiped her hand across her neon pink pantsuit. A small line of dirt smudged her otherwise perfect appearance. The scowl on her face grew slightly deeper.

"Your meeting was at three, Mr. Winston. I'm afraid we will have to make this fast."

Mikeis motioned toward the chairs. "Mind if I sit?"

Principal Walsh moved her head as she examined Mikeis. Imani couldn't be sure, but she thought she saw a look of disgust on the principal's face. It reminded her of when her grandma served venison and she had to suffer quietly through the meal. Principal Walsh finally nodded after what was obviously an excessive amount of time.

"So, Mr. Winston, what can I help you with?"

Imani looked at her dad. His skinny frame sank deep into the chair. His hand rubbed at his unkempt facial hair. "Well, ma'am," Mikeis leaned backward, "to put it frankly, my daughter has been getting bullied, and nobody seems to be doing anything about it.

The principal glared at Mikeis. She moved her gaze to Imani, blasting lasers through them both with her stare. Imani recoiled. This was what she was afraid of. She repositioned herself in the chair, again fidgeting with the shirt she felt was too tight.

"Well, that's very unfortunate. As I'm sure you're aware, we have a no-bullying policy at this school." The principal literally stuck her nose in the air. Imani thought the old woman was trying to look regal or sophisticated, but she only managed to look like a pompous bitch.

"So I've heard." Imani noticed her father's sarcastic tone and hoped the principal missed it. "Anyway. . ." Mikeis leaned forward in his chair. His elbows rested on his knees, and his hands held up his exhausted-looking face. "She's being bullied by your football team, and it needs to come to an end."

"I see." Principal Walsh dragged the words out. "And just what exactly are you accusing the boys of?" Principal Walsh exaggeratedly raised her eyebrows.

Her father tapped Imani on the shoulder. "Go ahead, baby," he encouraged.

Imani placed her hands firmly in her lap. She started to speak but realized she was staring at the floor. Lessons from her father about exuding confidence came flooding back to her, and she adjusted her gaze to meet the principal's eyes, inhaling deeply.

"It started off minor, ma'am. Some of the boys made faces at me, calling me stinky or fat, that kind of thing. They would pretend the earth trembled as I walked by. Just harmless dumb jock stuff. I ignored it mostly. But about three months ago, Lemichael asked me on a date."

Principal Walsh cleared her throat. "Lemichael?"

Imani shot her father a glance. He nodded.

"Lemichael Sanders."

Principal Walsh made a noise that sounded like an affirmative, and Imani took that as an invitation to continue.

"Well," she paused, "I'm not interested in him like that. I politely turned him down. He called me a—" She glanced at her father again, and again he nodded. "He called me a fat, nappy-headed bitch." It surprised Imani to see the principal hold her stoic look. She didn't flinch at a student swearing in her office like Imani had expected her to. "Things got worse from there. A couple of the boys stole my math homework and ripped it up. I tried explaining to Mr. Selmon why I didn't have the assignment, but he didn't believe me. Then I started getting aggressive texts from numbers I don't have saved in my phone."

Principal Walsh held up one bony finger. "What kind of texts?"

"At first, it was just words. I'd get a text here or there calling me a bitch or a whore. I just ignored them. Then one of them sent me a picture of their, uh, their anus."

Principal Walsh's stoic gaze faltered slightly. Imani saw the corner of her mouth tremble. She couldn't decide if the idea of a football player's anus appalled her or if she was trying to stifle a laugh.

"Eventually, I started receiving pictures of someone's penis. I don't think those were of Lemichael, though."

Any suggestion of humor faded from Principal Walsh's face. She leaned over her desk. "And why is that?"

"Because it's a white guy."

"I think it's the kid they call Irish," her father's deep voice boomed, startling Imani. Explaining the past few months of bullying gave her tunnel vision. She had nearly forgotten her father was in the room.

"Is that all?"

Imani and her father shared a glance. "What more do you need?" her father asked.

"Well, right now I'm hearing about a girl who is receiving texts and photos. She doesn't know for sure who is sending them. This is also the first I've heard about anyone sabotaging homework. This isn't what we would call," she paused, "actionable." She emphasized the word to drive the dagger home.

Hot tears swelled in Imani's eyes. She pulled her shirt lower to obscure her belly and began to stand up, but her father placed a hand on her arm. Fury swirled in his eyes. She slid back into the chair, awaiting the explosion that was sure to come. The three sat in silence for a few moments. Her father's lips were moving. He reminded her of a boxer after getting hit for the first time in a fight; his face clenched up like he was bracing for the next punch.

"Ma'am." Imani flinched at the sound of his voice. It lacked the friendly tone he had projected when he entered the office. "I'm not trying to question you or how you do your job, but my daughter needs your help."

The principal tossed her hands in the air and shook her head. "It's simply not actionable, Mr. Winston."

"Ma'am."

Principal Walsh raised her hand. "I'll talk to Coach Chevy about it, but I can't promise anything."

Her father's hands gripped the armrests of his chair, his knuckles turning white. Imani braced herself and prayed it wouldn't be too bad.

"I wasn't finished speaking, ma'am," her father said through gritted teeth.

Principal Walsh stood up. Her chair slid back across the floor. She moved around her massive desk and toward the door, opening it and stepping aside.

"Maybe next time you'll be on time," she said through a fake smile.

Imani was sure her father would throw his chair through the window or slam his hands on the principal's desk, but he did neither. He patted his thighs and stood up. He walked toward the door but stopped before walking through it. Imani looked back at the clock: three twenty-one. The principal had given them four minutes of her time. Four fucking minutes.

"Come on," her father commanded. Imani could see into the front office. Several people turned their heads toward the commotion. "This cunt doesn't give a fuck about us." Principal Walsh's mouth fell open. She attempted to say something, but the shock was too much. She stammered idiotically as Mikeis turned and walked out of the office. Imani scrambled to her feet and ran after her father, a massive grin stretched across her face. She slid her arm into her father's and walked beside him as they exited the front office.

Behind them, Principal Walsh shouted something about banning him from school property. She followed it up with something about nobody talking to her like that. With flawless execution, her father shot up the middle finger from over his shoulder just before the office door slammed shut.

Chapter 7

Justin shut the door and slammed the deadbolt into place. Chase hadn't thought anything about there being only one door to the cabin when they first arrived. It was a problem he was acutely aware of now.

Lemichael was the first to act after Justin handled the door. He rushed around the recliner, grabbing it around the sides and sliding it across the floor. The metal legs dug into the ground, scratching the wood floors and releasing an ear-piercing squeal. The scraping noise sent a shudder down Chase's spine. Lemichael angled the chair and wrestled with it for a moment before successfully wedging the back under the door handle.

The other boys stood lined up against the window, frozen in the exact spot they had been when the men hacked Ford to pieces. Lemichael turned and clapped his hands. The abrupt noise snapped Chase from his daze.

"Hector, Nick, and Chase," he pointed to each of them. "Help me block the window with the couch. Justin and Irish, check the phones for signals and call my dad." With Lemichael and Nick's dad being the chief of police, Chase wasn't surprised he was taking the lead.

The teammates jumped into overdrive and rushed to complete their respective assignments. Chase's head felt cloudy; he couldn't seem to wrap his mind around the reality of what just happened. Ford being slaughtered came to him in frozen images, playing in his mind like a slideshow instead of a video. An image flashed of a machete rising into the air and slinging blood in all directions. The next image was Ford's face as he begged for his life. Chase must have zoned out because Lemichael snapped his fingers a few inches from his face.

"You still with me, man?"

Chase nodded his head quickly and lifted his end of the couch. They worked as a team to move the couch, heavy from the mechanics of the built-in recliners, under the window. Despite years of weight training, the adrenaline coursing through his veins left Chase feeling shaky and numb. They slammed the couch into place and realized the back of the couch only covered about a quarter of the window.

Lemichael pointed toward the loveseat. "Let's stack them." Feeling returned to Chase's fingers when he grabbed the loveseat. With a collective grunt, the boys heaved the loveseat onto the couch and flipped it over in the process. The two fit together like Legos. The metal track of the loveseat's base pointed upward, like a rabbit's ears.

"There's no service out here," Justin shouted from the dining room.

"I got nothing either," Irish shouted, panic resonating in his voice.

Justin paced at the far end of the living room. His hands on his head, he yanked at his hair. "What the fuck was that?" he shouted. "He's fucking dead!"

Something moved in Chase's periphery. Before he could turn his head, there was a knock on the window. The boys lurched backward, away from the freshly stacked couches. The couches obscured the entire window from view, save for a few inches at the top. They could see plastic rabbit ears, speckled with blood, poking out from above the couch.

The boys scrambled away from the window. Hector tumbled to the floor. Nick and Lemichael nearly trampled him as they retreated. Chase reached under Hector's armpits and wrapped his arms around his chest. He heaved Hector's weight upwards and helped him to his feet. The two nearly tripped and fell again as they shuffled past the end table.

"Weapons!" shouted Justin. "We need weapons." His voice trembled.

The boys looked around for weapons. Justin ran into the kitchen. Chase couldn't see him, but he could tell from the sound of drawers being thrown open and slammed shut that he was searching for knives. Chase contemplated how even now, besieged by masked murderers, Justin remembered to close the drawers.

"I got knives," Justin cheered. He emerged from the kitchen holding a large knife in each hand. He handed one of the knives to Irish as he passed him. Irish's knuckles whitened from his grip on the handle.

Hector flipped the coffee table over so the top rested flat on the ground. He stepped onto it and methodically kicked each leg. They fell away from the table with ease. He picked up the broken legs and, one by one, handed them to Nick, Lemichael, and Chase.

Chase gripped the bottom of the leg and turned it over in his hand. The top of the leg, where it connected to the table, was square and made of solid wood. Two bent nails protruded from the makeshift club. It wasn't a machete, but it would have to do.

A tap on the kitchen window diverted their attention. They could hear the previously unnoticed drip of the kitchen faucet. Outside the front door, the floorboards creaked. Another tap rang out from the kitchen window. The boys crept into the kitchen behind Justin and Irish. They walked with their weapons at the ready.

Justin froze as he turned the corner into the kitchen. Chase stretched his neck and stood on his tiptoes to get a better look. Another masked assailant looked back at him through the kitchen window. The man's head was tilted slightly to the left; a single drop of blood ran down the mask from the right eye. Chase thought the rabbit could have been crying blood, but he knew whose blood it was. The man slowly cocked his head in the opposite direction. A grotesque display of bodily fluids coated his jumpsuit.

The man raised his blood-soaked right hand and gave that same wave. Hand flat, four fingers wriggling up and down.

A lump formed in Justin's throat. He pressed his left hand against Irish, pushing him away from the kitchen. The boys clumsily backed away.

"What are we going to do?" Hector whispered.

"Nothing," Justin snapped. "We're going to stay right here in the living room."

Lemichael shook his head. "Fuck no, bro. We have to get the fuck out of here."

"We can't, man. Those fucking psychos are out there," Justin protested.

Lemichael grabbed Justin's arm. "They could bust in through the windows at any minute."

Irish held his hands up, the knife displayed prominently in his right. "Who the fuck are they?" He looked around the huddle as each person shrugged or shook their head.

"Look, Chief Sanders will come looking for us if we wait here. We just have to wait it out," Justin insisted.

"I'm not sure I can just sit here for two more nights," Irish said.

A scraping sound filled the room. Chase swirled around, searching for the source. It came again from the opposite direction. Then again.

"They're dragging their machetes along the wall," Lemichael whispered.

Nick let out a sniffle, tears streaming down his face. "Are we just not going to talk about Ford?"

Justin shook his head. "Look, he was my best friend, but there's nothing. . ." He trailed off as a groan from outside cut him off. In unison, the boys jerked their heads toward the window. The groan repeated, louder this time. It sounded choked, like it was coming from underwater.

"Is that—" Chase allowed the sentence to drift off.

"Help me!" Ford's cry ripped through the night air. Every inch of Chase's flesh turned to goosebumps. His heart beat against his chest so hard it hurt. Ford began coughing. The sound of him clearing blood from his throat forced Chase to gag.

"Help me!"

Nobody moved.

"Please." Another cough and the sloshing sound of blood expelled from their dying friend's throat.

"We have to help him," Chase said.

None of the boys responded. "I don't want to die," Ford cried.

"Ok, ok, let me think," Justin said. "Ok, look, there are six of us and four of them. We go out there with our weapons. Two people grab Ford, and we drag him to the Jeep. We hoist him into the back, and we take the fuck off."

Lemichael shook his head. "Ford is three hundred and fifty pounds. We can't get him into the Jeep."

"I can," Chase stated. All eyes fixed on him.

"Justin! Nick! Someone help me. Please!"

Chase nodded. He locked a stern look into his face, trying to instill confidence in his older teammates. "I can carry him on my shoulders. I carried big guys when I wrestled back in Tampa. I just need someone to help me get him up the first time."

Justin grabbed Chase by the shoulders. The blade in his right hand came dangerously close to cutting his ear. "Are you sure?" There was a subtle crack in Justin's voice.

Chase nodded.

Justin looked around the group. He pointed to Lemichael, who just nodded. "Ok, we go out, Lemichael helps get Ford onto Chase's shoulders. Everyone defends Chase while he loads Ford into the Jeep. We all climb in and get the fuck out. Everyone good?"

The boys murmured their agreements in a series of "yeah" or "sure." They moved to the front door. Irish pulled the couch a few inches away from the window, allowing him to see outside. Chase tried to focus on controlling his breathing while they waited for the all-clear from Irish, a task he found much more challenging than he expected.

"I don't see them."

"On three," Justin whispered. Lemichael and Nick lifted the chair that blocked the front door, careful to make as little noise as possible. They took a few steps back and deposited the recliner to the side. Justin held up three fingers. He dropped the first one. He slid the deadbolt back before dropping his second finger. Chase took a deep breath. His heart raced. He could feel the rush of adrenaline coursing through his veins. This time it made him feel alive. His fight-or-flight instinct kicked in, and he was ready to fight. Justin dropped the last finger as he threw the door open.

Chapter 8

Megan had her face buried deep in Chase's hoodie; hot tears poured from her eyes and absorbed into the fabric. For a moment, the thought of him walking around the school with a wet imprint of her face on his chest created a rush of embarrassment. Her cheeks grew hot at the thought, but the feeling fled as quickly as it had come. Megan knew it didn't matter now what the other kids at school thought. She knew she wouldn't see them again after today.

Chase brushed his hand through her hair, allowing the brown locks to lace through his fingers. She asked him to rub her hair like this any chance they got; it made her feel special. But she didn't feel special now.

Her sobs slowed to a steady sniffling. Chase rested his hands firmly on her shoulders, and she knew he was about to pull her away. He would probably look her in the eyes and say something sweet. If he did, her sniffling would likely turn back into sobs. She wrapped her arms around him and buried her fingers into his back like claws. The desperate need to stretch the moment out as long as she could overwhelmed her. His grip on her shoulders loosened. Those powerful hands slid from her shoulders to her back, his powerful fingers digging deep into her muscles. The warmth from the friction spread across her upper back and into her shoulders.

"I didn't know," he whispered.

The words seemed to roll across the open expanse of the football field. Chase instructed her to meet him here when he found out, assuring her nobody went to the football field before school. According to Chase, it was the most secluded place on campus. Apparently, he liked to come here before school and enjoy the quiet or work on some last-minute homework. He promised it would be the perfect place for such an important meeting.

But now that she was here, standing in her boyfriend's arms, she felt like it exposed them to the world. There was nowhere for them to hide, nothing to obscure them from view. In this empty high school football stadium, their words and her sobs seemed to race up the bleachers and trumpet in all directions.

"I didn't know," he repeated. His voice was weaker this time. The hint of a sniffle chased the words.

"I know." Her voice was shaky.

He ran one of his hands through her hair again. The edges of her mouth twitched and threatened a smile. Even at her worst, Chase knew how to make her smile. She stifled the thought; this was no time for smiling.

They found out about the sex tape at the same time. Their phones didn't connect the first time they called because each had called the other at the exact same time. It took several tries for her call to go through, presumably because he finally quit trying to call her simultaneously.

He pushed her away and held her at arm's length. She watched as he looked her over, his eyes examining her from head to toe. That exposed feeling grew stronger. She longed for him to embrace her again. For his arms to block her vision. When their eyes met, the sob she was trying to hold back escaped. She did her best to put on a brave face.

He turned away from her and grabbed one of her hands. "Come on," he said, dragging her toward the home team's sideline benches. The two walked together, Chase slightly ahead. It reminded her of a Pinterest picture of a boyfriend dragging his love to some far-off, magnificent view. Under normal circumstances, she would do everything to savor this romantic snapshot in her mind. But these were not normal circumstances, and her feet felt heavy. The bench seemed to be a looming presence. She feared the conversation she was about to have. Her heart ached for the moments they had shared just a minute ago. She wasn't ready to face the consequences of their actions.

Chase sat down first. Compared to Megan, his massive frame took up a good portion of the bench. He patted the seat beside him, and she lowered herself onto the bench. Full of anxiety, she wrapped her arms around herself and rubbed the backs of her arms. Chase dropped one of his enormous arms around her, giving her a gentle pull. She allowed herself to fall into his chest, her ear landing over his heart. She embraced the moment, listening to the rapid beating.

"I asked Justin about the sex tape. He said he doesn't know who put the camera in there."

Megan tilted her head to look up at her boyfriend. From this angle, she could still see some of his boyish features. His jaw was square but soft. His brown facial hair was starting to come in, but it was patchy and uneven. She wished she could still be with him when he finished puberty because she knew he would be a heartthrob.

"And you believe him," she squeaked.

"He doesn't have much of a reason to lie, and if he had made the video, why post it?"

He lowered his head. Her heart skipped a beat when their eyes met. The mask of sadness on his handsome face and the anguish in his eyes caused her physical pain. She returned her gaze to her feet, unable to look at him any longer.

"I don't know, Chase. But we did it in his bedroom. It had to be his camera setup on the desk."

"I asked him for permission first. The guys on the team said lots of people have sex in there during Justin's parties."

Megan winced at the word sex. It conjured up an image of her parent's disapproving faces as the tape played on her mother's laptop. She knew it was immature, but she preferred phrases like "making love," or simply "it."

"Either way, my dad said it's natural, and we shouldn't be ashamed of it. I told him I loved you." His voice trailed off at the last part. Her heart should have skipped a beat at hearing the "L" word leave his mouth, especially for the first time, but she knew it would only make this next part that much harder. "My dad said he would notify the police," Chase continued. "We're minors, so making that tape was against the law."

Megan shook her head. "It doesn't matter now." Chase placed one of his large hands under her chin and gently tilted her head up. She tried to avert her eyes. Her body began to tremble again. Those heaving sobs she worked so hard to resist were returning.

"What do you mean?"

Tears rolled down Megan's face again. She was mad she couldn't stop them, mad she hadn't run out of tears by now. "My parents are religious, Chase."

He shook his head. Megan watched as the realization of what was coming washed over his face. His eyes glinted; Megan could see tears forming. Defiance overtook the look of concern on his face. She knew he was going to fight the inevitable. "My mother hasn't talked to me since they found out. Whoever did it sent her a copy of the video." The tears flowed faster. They raced down her cheeks, fell from her chin, and pooled in her lap.

Chase's mouth opened to speak but closed without a word.

"She, uh," Megan searched for the strength to say the words, "she talked to our priest."

Chase shook his head slowly. He mouthed the word "no," and Megan wondered if he had actually meant to say it out loud.

"They're sending me away. I'm going to stay with my aunt in Maine."

Megan watched a tear roll down Chase's face. His features transformed from that half-man, half-boy look that puberty brings to that of a defeated child. The look reminded her of a scolded puppy. "Will we still get to see each other? Can I call you?" Chase's voice was the one cracking now.

Megan shook her head. "My mom is taking my phone away. They won't let me come back till after high school." Chase buried his face in his hands. He tried to hide his tears, but when he looked back at her, his reddened eyes gave him away.

"My mother said that I can write to you. Old school. Traditional letters. My aunt has to screen them first, but she will allow us to do that."

Chase nodded. He took her hand in his. A comforting rush of warmth tingled up her arm at his touch. "Whatever it takes to stay in contact with you," he said. His reddened eyes fixed on hers. "I'll write to you all the time, I swear."

Megan forced a smile.

A car horn blared and pierced their solitary existence. They jerked their heads toward the road. Megan's mom parked her car on the side of the road along the stadium's north side. She sat in the driver's seat of her bright red Toyota Camry; a large wooden cross dangled from the rearview.

"I have to go." She stood up.

"Wait." Chase grabbed her arm. She turned back to face him.

"I love you."

She smiled through a veil of tears.

"I love you too."

Hesitantly, she started walking toward her mom's car. About ten feet away, she looked at him over her shoulder. She needed to tell him.

"My mom told me not to say anything to you."

A confused look washed over Chase's face.

"I'm pregnant, Chase."

Before he could respond, she turned away from him and ran toward her mother's car. It took all of her willpower not to look back. She couldn't allow herself to see the bewilderment on his face. The pain lingering in his eyes would ruin her.

Her sobs grew more intense as she approached her mother. They became increasingly uncontrollable with each step, until she collapsed into the passenger seat in a mess of tears and snot.

Her mother lingered, staring through the windshield at her daughter's defiler. Without a word, her mother put the car in gear and sped off down the road.

Chapter 9

The boys erupted through the open door and onto the cabin's front porch. They sprinted across the wooden planks, the echoes of their stomping feet blasting into the surrounding woods. Chase scanned the area around them as they rushed off the porch and across the open patch of dirt. The front end of the Jeep poked out from the side of the building, barely visible from his vantage point. Doing some quick calculations, he guessed it was about twenty yards from Ford's mangled body to the front of the Jeep. Chase knew he would have to get around to the back of the Jeep with Ford's enormous body. He tacked on another couple of yards to his estimation; with almost no help, he would need to lift Ford's three-hundred-and-fifty-pound body onto his shoulders and carry the behemoth twenty-five feet before depositing him in the back of the Jeep. Chase's confidence waned with every step toward the heap of maimed flesh of their teammate.

They reached Ford with no issues. Justin and Irish took defensive positions between Ford and the tree line. Their kitchen knives glinted in the moon's glow. Nick and Hector stood behind Chase and Lemichael, holding their makeshift clubs up like baseball bats.

Chase only had a moment to appreciate how ridiculous they must look before diving into his assigned duty.

Heavy Florida air clung to their shirts and skin. Chase sucked in a deep breath. The humidity was stifling. Bending down, he grabbed one of Ford's arms; he grasped his wrists and pulled. The skin on Ford's mangled arm separated from the bone, causing Chase's grip to slip immediately, and he went tumbling backward. His ass hit the dirt first, sending a painful shockwave rippling up his spine. He released an audible groan.

"Hurry up," Lemichael commanded. In the moonlight, Chase could see the red liquid coating his hands. Then the realization hit him. This was going to be even more challenging than he imagined.

"Oh fuck," Justin yelled. Chase snapped his head in that direction. Three men emerged from the trees, stopping just outside of the tree line. Ford's blood still coated their jumpsuits and caked their rabbit masks. The machetes dangled from their right hands. Blood dripped from the blades, pooling in sickly puddles at their feet. The men didn't approach; they didn't even seem to breathe. They stood in their spots, heads cocked slightly to the side, watching the boys through the mesh eyes of the bunny masks.

Chase scrambled back to his feet. He locked both hands around one of Ford's arms, digging his fingers deep into the remaining skin. "Push up on his back," he shouted at Lemichael. Lemichael positioned himself at Ford's head. He grabbed hold of the bloody shoulders and grunted as he raised him up. Ford's head flailed about uselessly. Chase would have assumed Ford was dead if it wasn't for his shallow breathing. Blood splatter ejected from his teammate every time he exhaled, painting Chase's face in red speckles.

"Hurry up!" Irish shouted. Chase allowed himself a quick glance in that direction. The three men hadn't moved an inch.

Lemichael and Chase managed to get Ford into a sitting position. Chase gagged at the putrid smell that wafted up from Ford's eviscerated stomach. Brown liquid seeped from exposed organs and intermingled with the coagulated pools of blood. Chase wasn't a doctor, but he could recognize where the stench was coming from. He knew Ford had a perforated bowel. He forced down the bile building in his throat.

"Oh shit," Nick called. The other boys stopped what they were doing and looked in his direction. Two more masked figures appeared on the side of the cabin. They walked a few feet and stopped. Machetes dangled from their hands as well. These men were clean, no sign of blood on them. Chase's heart thudded against his chest. There were more of them.

"Push," Chase ordered. He moved around to Ford's side and squatted as low as possible. The edges of his ass brushed the dirt as he pulled Ford's shredded arm over his shoulders. A warm sensation flowed down Chase's back. Lemichael groaned as he continued pushing the limp body forward. Chase inched Ford's massive frame onto his shoulders.

He summoned a deep, barbaric cry as he stood up. It was the yell of a weight lifter or an ancient Viking war chant. Ford's limp body lay across Chase's shoulders, blood flooding from his open wounds and coating Chase in a deep shade of red. The smell of feces permeated the air as Ford's open bowels evacuated onto Chase's back. He forced back a gag.

"Let's go!" His shout sounded weak, even to his own ears. Incredible weight pressed down on him, making it difficult to breathe and nearly impossible to talk.

Chase began his labored journey to the Jeep, watching the masked figures near the tree line as he walked. The teammates kept a steady pace, walking in unison. The rabbit-masked men walked at a slow pace behind the boys, maintaining the same distance the entire time.

Justin pressed buttons on the Jeep's key fob. Nothing happened. He kept pressing it with no response.

"They're following us," someone shouted. The blood building up in Chase's ears muffled everything. Ford's weight strained every muscle in his body and fire ripped through Chase's legs with each labored step.

Ten yards now, Chase encouraged himself. Justin and Irish kept pace ahead of him. He could feel Lemichael to his right and hoped the others were right behind him. The muscles in his lower back burned; his knees shook under the pressure of their combined weight. His right foot caught a rock, causing him to lose his balance. He stumbled forward before falling to one knee. His right knee bounced off the rocks, sending a shot of pain soaring through his lower body. Despite the weight and Ford's gore drenching him, he could sense the flow of blood gushing from the newly opened wound on his knee. Lemichael was quick to wrap his arms around Chase's chest, squeezing with all of his might, trying to hold Chase in place. That was probably the only thing that prevented Chase from lurching forward and face-planting. Chase slowly stood back up, regained his footing, and continued his trek toward the Jeep.

A scream filled the air as the boys rounded the side of the Jeep. Next to the driver's door was a sixth masked man, walking toward them at a steady pace, his machete raised high in the air.

"Oh, shit. Oh, shit," Irish repeated.

Justin and Irish began to back pedal. The two seemed to lose all sense of direction and distance as they ran into Chase. The jarring hit caused Ford's weight to shift backward, and in near slow motion, Chase fell. He had the momentary sense of his feet leaving the ground before the air expelled from his lungs. He lay half on Ford, half on the ground, and gasped for breath. Chase could hear the pattering of feet around him. He was distantly aware of his friends abandoning him, the sounds of their footsteps growing fainter the further they ran. He could feel the back of his head sinking deeper into Ford's open stomach. Another gut-wrenching gag formed, and at that moment, he realized he could no longer hear Ford's heart beating. The blood no longer pumped from the various open wounds on the giant boy's body, no more breaths rasping between his slashed lips.

Above him, the night sky appeared majestic, stars stretched as far as he could see. The moon shone boldly from behind several clouds. The fuzzy outline of rabbit ears entered his vision. As the masked man approached, the paralysis that had a grip on Chase's body released, and he was no longer frozen in place.

He scrambled to his feet; only a yard stood between him and one of the masked men. The attacker moved slowly with the confidence of a man on a mission. Another scream tore through the night air. Chase jerked his head to see Nick on the ground, gripping his right leg. Despite the poor lighting, Chase could see something sticking out of Nick's leg. The bushes rustled as a seventh man emerged from his hiding place. This man was still pulling his mask down over his face, allowing Chase to glimpse the salt and pepper stubble on the man's jawline before he had the mask down completely. This man carried a bow in his left hand, and a quiver of arrows hung from his right hip.

Instinctually, he moved away from this man, tripping over Ford in the process. His head smacked on the ground for the second time in as many minutes. Fighting unconsciousness, he pushed himself up and kept moving. Near the door, he could make out the images of Justin and Irish pulling Lemichael into the house. Lemichael was staring at his brother, who was rolling around in the dirt, pleading for his friends to save him. Irish and Justin gripped Lemichael around the waist and shoulders, and he allowed his friends to pull him into the cabin.

Everything seemed muffled and in slow motion. Chase wasn't sure if it was from adrenaline, the copious amount of alcohol, or the two possible concussions he had just suffered. Every fiber of his being begged him to give in to exhaustion and pain, but he pushed on.

Without thinking, he sprinted toward Nick. Nick was already crawling toward the cabin, dragging his damaged leg behind him. When he reached his friend, he could clearly see the back of an arrow poking up from Nick's right knee. The boy continued to scream in pain each time he pulled himself forward.

Chase squatted down like a defender scooping up a fumble and grabbed Nick under one arm. He summoned every ounce of strength he had left, lifting Nick to his feet. Nick draped his arm over Chase's shoulder. The pair managed to take just a single step before one of the masked men appeared from nowhere. He stood like a blockade between them and the cabin. The rabbit mask shifted slightly, betraying the smile forming beneath it.

The masked man held up one of Ford's severed fingers and wagged it at Chase.

"Tsk. Tsk. Tsk," the masked man said from behind the rabbit's mouth.

The boys in the cabin weren't screaming anymore. Over the masked man's shoulder, Chase could make out the frantic faces of his friends through the window. Hatred boiled through him as he watched Justin slam the door shut.

The remaining six masked men walked toward him from all directions. Nick squeezed his hand. Beneath his blood and feces-soaked shirt, Chase's skin felt icy. The man's voice sent shock waves through his veins.

"Don't leave me," Nick whispered as he slumped back to the ground.

The light from the cabin illuminated the area around them. There was no avenue of escape; the attackers had boxed them in.

With nothing left to do, he closed his eyes and prayed.

"Our Father, who—"

"Stop," the masked man demanded. For some reason, Chase had expected the voice to sound demonic or evil, but to his surprise, it sounded like a regular middle-aged man. Chase opened his eyes. The masked man in front of him stepped aside, opening a path to the cabin.

Chase looked from the man to Nick. Nick's face begged Chase not to leave him. He grasped at Chase's pant leg as he stepped forward, but Chase pulled his leg forward and out of Nick's grasp.

"I'm sorry, Nick."

"No."

"I'm so sorry." Chase turned his back on Nick and the masked men and walked toward the cabin.

"N-no," Nick stuttered behind him. Chase wasn't sure if Nick was talking to him or the masked men. He supposed it didn't matter anymore.

"I'll fucking kill you. I swear to god. I'll fucking—" Nick never finished the sentence. An ear-shattering scream filled Chase's ears. The sloshing sound of blood followed the scream, the sound of splatter going all directions.

Chase didn't look back, but he could tell the masked men were giving Nick the same treatment they had given Ford. As he stepped onto the porch, he heard a sound like a tree limb breaking. Chase knew it was a big bone, maybe a femur, snapping. He walked slowly across the porch and to the front door. Nick's screams were already growing weaker. Chase was grateful he didn't beg the way Ford had; the last words he heard from Nick were some sort of insult. He couldn't make out the exact sentence over the sloshing of blood and the smacks of the machetes, but he was sure Nick had told the man to do something to his own mother.

He turned the handle and pushed. It didn't budge. In a trance-like stupor, he calmly knocked on the door. A commotion erupted on the other side, and he could hear the distinct sound of furniture legs scraping across the floor. The lock on the door clicked, and the door flung open. Hector held the door ajar, tears streaming down his face. Chase could see little chunks of vomit on his chin. Chase wondered if he was crying; he felt nothing except the sticky sensation of Ford's blood drying on him.

Stealing a last glance, he turned his head back to the group of masked men. Nick, or what was left of him, lay in the middle of the men. They had reduced his carcass to a heap of viscera. Stringy sinew clung to the murderer's blades. White bones protruded through patches of torn skin. The bloody stump of Nick's severed left leg stuck straight into the air.

A familiar burning rose in the back of Chase's throat. He turned to the side and launched a stream of vomit onto the porch. When he finished, he saw the men staring at him through their blood-soaked rabbit masks.

He wiped the vomit from his lips and replaced it with the blood that stained his arm. He walked through the open door and into the living room. The door slammed shut behind him, followed by the scratch of the furniture being pushed against the door. He was already sick of that routine.

"Why'd you leave him?" Lemichael's voice boomed as he approached.

"Why'd you leave him?" Lemichael demanded again. He grabbed Chase by his fluid-soaked shirt. Chase didn't resist as Lemichael shook him violently. "You left him! You left him!"

Justin and Irish were trying to pull Lemichael off of him. His shirt ripped, exposing the gruesome realization that the fluids had soaked through his shirt and painted his chest in a swirl of red and brown.

Something snapped inside Chase at that moment. His heart rate fluctuated throughout this experience, but it was hard and steady now. He looked up to meet Lemichael's stare. Something like recognition flashed in Lemichael's eyes just as Chase's fist connected with his face. Lemichael collapsed to the ground, taking the rest of the shirt with him. Chase raised his fist and brought it down on Lemichael again. He hit him a third time before someone grabbed his arm, and he felt himself being lifted. The remaining boys were on him now, forcing him back into the wall.

"Chill, man. Chill out."

It was Hector's voice.

He pushed himself off the wall with his other hand and pushed Hector to the floor. He turned toward Lemichael. His left eye ballooned, and a shade of blue filled the area around his nose. Chase pointed a finger at himself; the veins in his neck protruded.

"Why'd I leave him?" he shouted. "Why'd I leave him?" His voice raised octaves each time he spoke. He turned his finger toward Lemichael. "Where the fuck were you? That's your brother out there!" He pointed toward the window. "Why am I the only one covered in his blood?"

Chase shook his head and collapsed against the wall, every muscle in his body convulsing uncontrollably. He allowed himself to slide to the ground, leaving a smear of blood and shit on the wall. He rocked back and forth as the other boys struggled to lay a barely conscious Lemichael on the couch.

"You all left us out there," Chase's voice quivered.

He raised his head to see the other boys looking at him. He wiped the tears and snot from his face.

"You left us to die."

Chapter 10

Katie watched through the windshield of her car as her father smoked a cigarette. He leaned against a tree at the end of the parking lot; his grayish shirt seemed to blend in with the trunk. The cigarette rolled between two pinched fingers before being buried into his lips. A cherry red tip burned bright as he inhaled the toxic fumes deep into his lungs.

Kyle Simpson turned forty-two last week. Katie's mind drifted to an image of her father smiling from behind his homemade birthday cake, a pang of guilt stabbing at her heart. He looked older now, far older than his forty-two years, older than any man in his early forties should look. Black bags formed under his eyes, and a sickly yellow tint seemed to overtake the healthy tan complexion he had worn only a week ago. Even his clothes appeared disheveled. There was a ketchup stain on his shirt, and mud clung to his shoes. His stubble was growing out of control for a man who normally prided himself on a professional appearance.

"Are you even fucking listening to me?" Lemichael's voice exploded through the phone. Anger seethed from every syllable.

"Yeah, I'm listening." She meant for her words to sound stoic, but to her, they sounded hollow. She watched her father toss his smoked cigarette aside. He reached into his pocket and withdrew the pack of Newports, smacking the pack against his hand three times before he relented and dug his finger into the box in search of his next nicotine fix. She glanced down at the floorboard and the three empty packs at her feet. She looked back at him. A fresh cigarette retrieved, he pressed the cancer stick to his lips and flicked his lighter. She gently shook her head; he had almost quit for real this time.

"So you're doing it?"

She cranked up the air conditioning in the car. The thermostat on the corner of the radio told her it was ninety-five degrees outside, but the air inside the car was stifling, like a weight was compressing her chest. With every word Lemichael spoke, another pound was added.

"I don't know if I can," her voice quivered. Her face became flushed with embarrassment. Her father's disheveled appearance disappeared behind a wall of tears.

"Listen to me, Katie. I'm not letting one night ruin my whole life. You need to take care of this shit."

She leaned her head against the headrest and punched the dashboard of her car. A single dent from her middle knuckle materialized when she removed her hand. Causing the imperfection felt good; if only it was Lemichael's face instead of her own car.

"Katie, you have to do this. We can't be parents."

She looked out the driver's side window at the white one-story building near the end of the parking lot. A line of pro-life protestors obscured most of the building. They displayed their homemade signs, hoisting them prominently into the air. Just like her father, the red letters on the building blurred.

Tall Oak Women's Clinic.

"Don't be a bitch about this, OK? Go take care of this, and we can return to being together." Lemichael's voice fluctuated from callous to caring in only two sentences.

"You said you loved me," she cried into the phone. She couldn't hold it back anymore. His heartless words broke the dam holding back the flow of tears. Shame flooded her body.

"I do, baby."

"Then why aren't you here with me?" Her words became an incomprehensible wail in her ears.

"You got to calm down, I can't understand you when you get all worked up. This ain't that big of a deal."

She dug her feet into the floorboard, the pressure radiating up her legs. "Not a big deal?" she shouted into the phone. "What kind of asshole says that to a person?"

"Ok, ok, I'm sorry, baby. I love you. I'm just scared right now." A softness overtook his tone. For a moment, just the briefest flash of a second, she felt that love for Lemichael come soaring back.

"You're scared, Lemichael? What about me? You don't think I'm scared?"

"I'm sure you are, but isn't your dad there with you?" The softness was gone again, replaced by defiance.

She looked back at her dad and watched him spark another cigarette.

He's going to smoke himself to death right here in the parking lot.

"Yeah, he's here, but you should be." Anger gnashed behind the last word.

"I had practice."

Her trembling hands nearly dropped the phone.

"Practice!?"

"Yeah, practice. You know how coach gets when we miss practice."

"I don't give a fuck about your fat fuck of a coach," she sobbed. Her sobs were growing stronger, and she hated herself for not being able to stop them. The fact Lemichael could hear her pain only made her angrier. And the worst part was, he didn't seem to care. She ground her teeth in an attempt to stifle the crying, the vibrations sending a wave of pain into her jaw. She thought about her mom, the woman who hated when people ground their teeth.

"I don't know if I can do it." Her words cut sharply between her wails.

Lemichael's end of the line was silent, save for a subtle rustling. "Hello?"

"Yeah," Lemichael said. His voice sounded even colder than it had earlier. "Listen, I didn't want to do this, but you better get that fucking abortion." Katie sat up straight in her seat. His words had gone from cold to hateful. Fear flooded her body.

"My dad's the chief. My best friend's dad is a deputy. My other best friend's dad is the mayor. We can make life miserable for your family. Now quit being a stupid cunt and get your ass into that clinic." He made sure to put emphasis on his command.

She pressed the end button on the phone before realizing what she had done. Frigid ice flowed through her veins. She glanced back at the thermostat - ninety-six degrees. Despite the heat, goosebumps now covered her skin.

She pushed open the car door and wiggled herself from the seat. Seeing her exit the vehicle, her dad tossed his half-smoked cigarette and walked across the parking lot. He wrapped one arm around her and leaned in close. The stench of his cigarettes intermixed with his body odor, creating a noxious fume.

"Are you sure this is what you want?"

She wanted to fake a smile, but the muscles around her mouth wouldn't cooperate. She just nodded.

"What did Lemichael say?"

She shook her head. The tears washed over her face again. "He's not who I thought he was, Daddy."

Her father pulled her into an embrace. His arms draped over her shoulders, and one of his hands rubbed the back of her head. She found herself stuck between needing her father's support and an overwhelming desire to gain some distance from that awful smell.

He released his hug, and she managed to gain some much-needed space. "Let's just get this over with," she said as she wiped the tears from her face.

Her father nodded. "Stay close to me until we're inside. Those religious nuts are protesting in front of the door."

The two ventured across the parking lot. The protestors chants grew louder as they approached. There were chants about God and babies. Covering her ears, she tried not to hear them. She swallowed hard, attempting to push down the guilt that was building up.

The pair emerged from the parking lot to face the enormous crowd, which stretched across the sidewalk in both directions. There were chants of "God loves you" and "repent for your sins.

A large man in a purple shirt with a massive golden cross taped on the front approached them. "You don't have to do this, young lady. God doesn't want this." The man's voice was gruff, and the whiskers of his mustache danced with each word. Her father attempted to shield her and push past the big man, but more protesters surrounded them. They begged and pleaded with her not to go through with the abortion. The twang of guilt in her chest ballooned to epic proportions.

Her father pulled her along, forcing their way through the crowd. The chants slowly turned from ones of love to shouts of hatred and disgust. The large man who had been the first to approach her called her a whore. Someone told her she would burn in hell. Their faces turned tomato red and engulfed her. Slurs and insults tore into her ears from all directions. She could hear her father shouting at the protesters to fuck off, but his words seemed distant. The crowd engulfed her in a wave of extreme zealotry, taunting her with every step.

Her father finally managed to push through the crowd of protesters, and they climbed the steps leading to the clinic's front door. A woman in scrubs stood beside the door, her black hair pulled into a tight bun. Her skinny hands beckoned her forward.

Katie sighed when they reached the nurse. Her hand rested on the door handle. Her father greeted the nurse, but the woman didn't open the door. She leaned in close to Katie and whispered, "This is your last chance to save your soul from hell."

Katie clenched her fists. "What the fuck did you just say to me?"

The woman started to repeat herself, but the door flung open. A large security guard emerged from the building and shouted at the fake nurse. Katie felt a tug on her arm as her father ushered her inside.

The inside of the clinic looked just like any other. A receptionist booth on one side, rows of chairs and a door in the corner where the nurses called the next patient on the other. She took a step toward the reception desk. Her father's grip on her arm stopped her.

"Is this what you want or what Lemichael wants?" His face was stern. His eyes flickered around the room.

"Lemichael," she cringed as his name left her lips, "he wants this."

Her father nodded. "And what do you want?" His words were full of nothing but love and compassion. She looked down at the floor, unable to meet his eyes.

"Katie?"

She shook her head again. "I want nothing to do with that asshole."

Her dad nodded. "Ok. You know I love you, right?"

"I love you, too, Dad."

"And you know I would do anything to protect you?"

"I'm protecting all of us, Dad."

She shook off his grip and walked away from her father. Approaching the counter, she glanced back to see a surprised look on his face, his hands firmly planted on his hips. He strutted across the room.

The receptionist was speaking, but her father raised a hand. "One moment, ma'am." Shock spread across the receptionist's face. He turned back to Katie.

"What do you mean you're protecting us?"

This time, she summoned the courage to look him in the eyes. "I think you know why."

She grabbed the clipboard from the receptionist and began filling in the answers to the many questions.

Chapter 11

The room went black.

"What the fuck," Hector yelped.

Somewhere in the darkness, the rapid click, click of the light switch being flipped reached their ears. "They cut the power," Justin whispered. He moved to the edge of the curtain to look outside. A shimmer of moonlight bled through the crack and illuminated his profile. "I can't see anything."

"What do we do?" Irish asked.

"I don't know, man. Maybe we just hide in here until help comes," Justin answered.

He returned the curtain to its place and launched the room back into complete darkness. Chase trembled in his position against the wall. Without warning, he jumped to his feet.

"I got to," he paused, and the other boys could hear him wrestling with his clothes, "got to get this off." His voice trailed off. His basketball shorts made a slopping sound when he tossed them to the floor. "I have his fucking blood on me," Chase howled. Panicked, he stumbled blindly through the house, looking for a towel. "I have to clean this off. Guys, help me clean this off." His voice was full of anxiety.

"Dude, shut the fuck up. You're too loud," Irish commanded.

"What? I'm too loud? Those fucking psychos know we're in here. It's not like we're hiding in here!"

With hands out before him, Justin walked across the room and shuffled his feet like a zombie. He worked his way around the furniture until he reached Chase. Justin gripped Chase's shoulders firmly. A warm, sticky liquid coated his hand.

"I know, bro, but let's just be quiet anyway."

Chase nodded, then realized nobody could see him in the dark. "Yeah, okay."

Justin turned toward the others. "OK, let's get the knives and clubs and go to the bedroom. It's a smaller room; it puts one more door between us and those assholes. We can defend it better."

"Yeah, I like that," Irish said. "Hector, help me pick up Lemichael."

"One second, man, I think I'm going to be sick," Hector said. "We shouldn't have gotten so fucking drunk."

"Shit, man, it's not like we knew fucking psychos were coming after us," Irish replied.

"You two shut up and grab him, please." Justin released Chase's shoulders.

Irish and Hector shuffled through the dark. They took up a position on either side of their half-conscious friend.

"I'm sorry, Lemichael. I shouldn't–" Chase stopped when Justin put his hand back on his shoulder.

"Not right now," Justin said.

Hector whispered to Irish to pick their friend up on the count of three. He never made it past two. The clanking sound of metal interrupted their count. The sound rang out through the night air.

"They're hammering something," Chase whispered.

Justin shuffled back to the window and peered outside. "I can't see anything," he whispered.

The clang of the hammer beating down on something continued for about thirty seconds before stopping. Chase shuffled to the window and looked out the side opposite Justin. Darkness enveloped the area in front of the cabin. Slivers of moonlight shone through the clouds and snaked their way through the trees. From the slight moonlight, he could make out the silhouette of a man dragging something.

"I see something," Chase said.

Hector and Irish appeared by his side and stretched their necks for a look. The silhouette of a masked man stopped at the base of a tree. Two more silhouettes appeared by his side. They seemed to materialize from the darkness like apparitions. The two men lifted something off the ground. The little moonlight that knifed through the trees glinted off the metal head of a hammer as the third man lifted it above his head.

He swung it toward the tree. Chase expected to hear that same metallic clang he had heard previously. Instead, Nick's screams filled his ears.

"Please! No! Oh, God! No!"

Chase watched as the shadowy figure brought the hammer down repeatedly. Each time, Nick washed the metallic clang out, begging for mercy. Chase could feel the frantic cries vibrating throughout his entire body. He felt cold again. His blood retreated from his extremities. Irish's weight pressed against his shoulder as the other boy also searched the window for an indication as to what was happening.

"What're they doing to him?" Hector asked.

The hammering stopped as suddenly as it started. Nick's moans were heartbreaking, reminding Chase of a trapped animal begging for freedom. They could do nothing as he repeatedly begged them, "Just kill me."

Chase squinted against the decreasing darkness. He could not distinguish the shapes of the masked men against the forest's still-deep shadows. Justin jumped at the sound of something being dropped closer to the cabin. He tried to make out just how far away the noise was, but before he could figure it out, a flood of light illuminated the tree line.

Chase gasped. He felt the pressure of Irish's body dissipate as the boy slumped away from the window, followed by a thud as he crashed to the floor.

Chase's mind put the image together piece by piece. Ford's large, dismembered body dangled from a tree. His arms stretched above his head, his hands resting one on top of the other, palms facing the cabin. The gray head of a nail protruded from a bloody hole in his hands. His entrails dangled like an open bag of ropes from the deep gashes in his abdomen. A grotesque concoction of bodily fluids pooled around his feet and coagulated into a soup. Nailed to his chest, a wooden sign prominently displayed the word "Rapist" in black paint.

Chase's eyes flicked toward Nick, who hung from the tree next to Ford. Unlike the former, Nick was still alive. He thrashed about like a trapped animal, chest moving up and down in rapid succession. The wooden sign nailed to his chest read "Abuser." Blood seeped from Nick's mouth.

Chase watched as a masked man emerged from between the two trees. One ear of his rabbit mask had cracked in half. Chase wondered if it had been like that earlier or if it happened in the commotion. The machete dangled from his right hand. Slowly, he raised his arm, pointing the bloodied, flesh-covered blade toward the sky. Bits of gore decorated the man's jumpsuit. He tilted his head slightly to the right and waved at the boys.

Chase wanted to scream, but the wind got trapped in his lungs. His mouth hung open in a mock shout. He tried to protest, but no words came.

The masked man turned the machete sideways. Nick stopped thrashing when he caught sight of the man. Tears streamed down the boy's face. His mouth moved, and even though Chase couldn't hear the words, he knew Nick was begging for his life. Chase watched as Nick's face morphed from one of desperation to a look of acceptance. The boy quit protesting and stared at the window, his eyes searching frantically for something.

The man swung the blade, and Nick stopped moving. He turned his back to the boys, his body obscuring their view. They could see the man's arm moving back and forth. The sawing probably lasted a few seconds, but to Chase, it lasted for minutes.

None of the boys moved. It was like a car wreck they couldn't look away from. Irish remained planted on the ground at Chase's feet. He rocked slightly from side to side, letting out the kind of groan someone would release when fighting back an illness. Hector sniffled in the blackness behind Chase. Justin breathed long, drawn-out breaths. Each exhale steamed the window.

Eventually, the man stopped sawing. He turned, holding Nick's severed head out. He slid his blade into the decapitated neck and held it high in the air. It reminded Chase of a football player holding up a trophy after a big win. A very fucked up trophy.

None of the boys noticed Lemichael approaching the window until he released a deep, painful wail. It snapped Chase from his trance. He grabbed Lemichael around the shoulders and forced his head down. He pulled him into a powerful embrace, but was met with punches to his back and ribs. The impacts stung his skin, but the punches themselves carried no actual weight. Chase squeezed tighter, trying to restrain him from hurting himself.

"Don't look," Chase whispered into Lemichael's ear. "Don't look."

"Let me go!" Lemichael fought to break away from Chase's grip. "I'll kill you. You hear me? You sick fuck! I'll rip you apart with my bare fucking hands!"

Spit flew from Lemichael's mouth. He swung his fist wildly against Chase. The punches lost power with each swing, and the boy's fury drained with each shout. He slumped into Chase, allowing Chase to support his full weight.

Chase lowered him to the ground. "Hey, hey, look at me," Chase commanded. He grabbed Lemichael under his chin. He jerked his head upward and forced Lemichael to meet his eyes. "We will make them pay, but we have to hold our shit together until then."

Chase could see Lemichael's face, whitewashed in the moon's pale glow. The boy's eyes glistened with tears. "They killed him. They killed my brother."

Justin appeared at their side. "We're going to filet those mother-fuckers." Justin slid his knife into Lemichael's hand.

He looked down at his hand. He nodded. "How?"

"Listen up," Justin started. "Grab what you can. We're still going to the master bedroom."

Chase stood up and looked out the window. The masked executioner had vanished. Nick's headless corpse still hung from the tree beside Ford's desecrated carcass.

The boys picked up their weapons and began shuffling toward the back bedroom when a knock on the front door caused them to stop dead in their tracks. Hector was closest to the door. He took a step toward it.

"No," Chase whispered. "Just come on."

The knocking continued. It sounded playful, reminding Chase of something his father would do before entering his room. Two rapid knocks, an exaggerated pause, and a final quick knock. Whoever was knocking continued this same pattern two more times.

Hector was the only one who moved. He took another silent step toward the door.

"Come on," Justin said.

Hector ignored him and took another step.

"Please," Chase begged.

Hector was at the door now. He rested his hands gingerly on either side of the peephole. He pressed his face against the door, straining his eyes against the narrow view.

"There's no one—" Hector started before an ear-shattering explosion cut him off. Hector's head jerked back in a violent, snapping motion. A hole opened in the back of his skull, painting the wall behind him with his brain matter. His body crumpled to the floor.

Chase instinctively covered his ears. Irish, Lemichael, and Justin sprinted past him and into the master bedroom. Chase lowered his hands, his ears ringing. He looked at the front door; a large hole replaced what had once been the peephole. He could see bits of a white rabbit mask peering in through it.

Acting on pure adrenaline, he rushed forward and grabbed Hector's arm. Straining against the boy's dead weight, he yanked him away from the front door and dragged him across the floor toward the master bedroom. A trail of brain matter spewed out behind Hector. Somewhere behind him, other boys screamed, but their words weren't forming coherent sentences in his head. He dragged Hector past a window and glimpsed his face in the moonlight. One of his eyes was completely missing. The gunshot replaced it with a hole full of tissue and shattered bones. His other eye rolled lazily to one side, completely void of life. Hector's jaw hung slack in a mockery of a scream.

Chase released Hector's lifeless arm, allowing it to thump to the floor. His balance waned, and he fell backward against the wall. He lay there dazed for a moment, listening to the sound of his friend's murderer knocking on the door. The knocks followed the same pattern as before, taunting them. He rolled onto his side and forced himself to his feet. Behind him, the door shook on its hinges.

Someone is kicking the door in, Chase thought. He sprinted down the hall and fell into the master bedroom. He crashed against the bed's footboard and flipped head-first onto the mattress. Justin slammed the door behind him and clicked the lock. The boys retreated backward, away from the door.

Chase swam through the comforter and fought back to his feet. Feeling around in the darkness of the room, his hands danced over a myriad of items. His fingers scrambled for purchase until they bumped into something large on the end table. He grasped it with both hands and yanked it up. The cord of the bedside lamp snapped as he pulled at it.

The front door burst open and hit the wall behind it. Footsteps raced around the cabin, echoing off the wooden floorboards and swirling around the walls. The boards moaned under the weight of their assailants.

"We're so fucked," Irish whispered.

Chapter 12

Kourtney pressed the shot glass to her lips and forced herself to tilt her head back and swallow the clear liquid. She expected the tequila to burn her throat as it went down, but the burning sensation subsided several shots ago. Her stomach did somersaults, and it took all of her willpower to force back a gag. She tucked her left thumb into her palm and squeezed it. She had heard from some of the girls on the cheerleading team that it helped control your gag reflex. She was pretty sure they were using it for something else but thought it was worth a shot in this scenario as well.

"I've never seen a chick who can keep up with us," Justin shouted above the music. Kourtney could barely hear him above the eighties hip hop but high-fived him anyway. Lemichael and Nick danced around Hector's kitchen, jokingly grinding on anyone who got too close.

It surprised her when she got invited to a party at Hector's house. Kourtney never considered herself to be one of the cool kids. She considered herself to be cool kid adjacent. Yes, she was a cheerleader, but not the cheer captain. Like so many of the girls at Tall Oak High, she had dated one of the football players last year, but he wasn't a starter. Still, when she got the text, her heart leaped at the opportunity. She immediately texted the other cheerleaders to confirm if any of them were going. A few hours later, she was riding in the backseat of a "pepto-pink" convertible with the other girls heading to Hector's party.

The invite was from Hector himself. She wasn't even sure how he had gotten her number. Maybe one of the other players, or maybe even a cheerleader, had given it to him. She didn't care either way; she was just grateful to be invited. The text said, "Hey, small party at my place tonight. Want to come?" It took an awkward exchange of texts to figure out who it was. Luckily, Hector was well adept at flirting, quickly recovering from the awkwardness.

Ford poured another shot of tequila into each of their glasses.

Kourtney held up her hand. "I don't think I can do another."

Hector put his arm around her. His biceps bulged as he pulled her close.

"The bottle's almost gone, babe. After a few more shots, we just chill for the rest of the night."

Kourtney's heart did a little stutter step when he called her babe. She nodded, lifted the glass to her lips, and downed the tequila. Again, she gagged.

"Alright, one more," Ford shouted.

Kourtney wasn't sure she could hold another shot down. The room seemed to be tilted slightly. She shook her head too aggressively, almost sending herself tumbling. "No, I'm done."

Hector flexed again, both pulling her in closer and helping to keep her standing. "Seriously," he begged, "one more?"

Grinning, she held up her finger. "One more, and that's it."

Hector flashed her a smile, forcing her heart to do another little flutter. Ford shoved another shot glass into her hand. It was so full that the natural shaking of her hands caused alcohol to spill over the edges. She inhaled sharply before downing her last shot. Quickly, she turned away from the group, afraid she was going to vomit. Hector rubbed her back as she hunched over the sink, desperately fighting her body's natural reaction. "You killed that shit," he said. The vibrations of the eighties-era hip-hop songs rocked her eardrums. The combination of the alcohol, blaring music, and her nervousness completely disoriented her. She attempted to steady herself, grasping for the sink. Inexplicably, her hands missed the counter, causing her to stumble and nearly fall down. At the last second, Hector caught her around her waist and hoisted her back to her feet.

"Whoa, you good?"

"Yeah, I'm good. I just need some water," she mumbled.

"Why don't you go lay down? You might just need to sleep it off," Hector suggested.

Kourtney could hear the other boys laughing through the loud music. She peeled herself from Hector's arms and leaned against the kitchen counter. Vomit threatened to erupt from her stomach. The room was completely spinning now; she could feel herself leaning to the left but couldn't stop herself from collapsing. One of the boys caught her before she hit the ground. She could no longer tell which boy it was. Her vision was rapidly becoming blurred, her words slurred, and her body grew numb.

"Where are my friends?" she asked.

"They went home," someone answered in a deep voice. The voices seemed muffled, like they were speaking through a pillow.

"I want to—" her voice trailed off. Her thoughts seemed cloudy and incoherent in her head. "Home," she said.

"Nah, that's not a good idea," Justin said as he entered her line of sight. Her blurry vision made it seem like his edges faded. "Why don't you go lay down in Hector's bed? We can come check on you in a bit."

Kourtney nodded her head. "I'm so tired."

Someone's arms wrapped around her and hoisted her into the air. She tried to lift her head to see which boy it was, but her head was too heavy, or maybe her neck was too weak. She couldn't be sure anymore. The floor faded from view as whoever had a hold of her carried her up the stairs. They reached the landing, and her head slumped forward. She wasn't able to control herself as her eyes rolled toward the ceiling.

She heard a thud as a door was kicked open, and light flooded out of a bedroom. She could see the blur of bedroom furniture swirl past as the boy carrying her whirled around. The boy didn't gently set her in bed like she would have expected him to. He simply let go. In her inebriated state, the fall lasted much longer than it should have.

She lay on the bed now, staring back up at the ceiling. Hector's face came into view. His features seemed soft through her blurred vision.

"You awake?" Hector asked. Kourtney tried to respond but only managed a gurgling noise.

"Relax, Hector. I've used this shit plenty of times," Justin said as he sauntered into the room.

"You sure, man? I don't want her waking up and remembering shit."

Kourtney tried to raise her head, but it remained glued to the pillows. Someone pulled her to the other side of the bed and yanked her shirt over her head. Panic tore through her as the realization of what was happening set in. Summoning every bit of strength she had left, she managed to roll onto her side before being forced back down to the bed.

"You sure she won't remember?" Hector asked again.

"Quit being a fucking pussy," Irish answered from outside Kourt-ney's blurry field of view.

There was a yank at her waist, and the feeling of cold air rushing over her nude body caused her flesh to break out in goosebumps.

"Alright, Hector, you're up first," Justin said.

She heard the clicking of a camera. Were they taking pictures? Hector climbed on top of her. His hot breath reeked of tequila. His body felt heavy on top of her, and she found it hard to breathe. She tried to push him off, but her hands brushed uselessly against his chest. She tried to protest as she felt the pressure building between her legs. Shamelessly, she allowed a tear to escape and roll onto the bed.

Blackness engulfed her vision, and she was grateful to be losing consciousness.

Kourtney awoke in her own bed with no recollection of how she got there. Her last clear memory was of doing a shot in Hector's kitchen. But despite the boys' best efforts, bits and pieces of the events that occurred later in the night popped up in her mind like movie clips. The memories were incomplete but horrible nonetheless. Hector's awful breath. Irish's red hair brushing against her cheeks. She remembered Lemichael, and Nick, and Ford. Worst of all, she remembered Justin. She remembered how he rolled her onto her stomach and had his way with her. His monstrous voice rang in her ears.

"Don't pretend you didn't want this," his words echoed repeatedly.

The memory released a surge of adrenaline. She shot up in bed, pain radiating from her groin into her abdomen. She smudged a lone tear across her face with a brush from the back of her hand.

She forced herself to her feet; the weight of her body sent knives stabbing into her. She limped to her desk and collapsed into her pink office chair. Shame washed over her as she pulled two sheets of paper from her spiral notebook. On the first, she wrote a letter to her best friend, Taylor. On the second, she wrote a letter to her parents. She folded the first letter into a little triangle. She wrote Taylor's name as they always did, making a heart where the O should be. Reaching over, she dropped this letter into her open underwear drawer and closed it. She left the letter to her parents flat on the desk and rested her pen across it.

She slid back her chair and stood up. Her movements felt hollow, as if outside of her control, robotic. Again, little knives stabbed her all over. She picked up her cell phone off the desk and crept across the hall. Entering the bathroom, she flicked on the lights.

Her reflection shocked her. Mascara coated her cheeks. Her hair was messy, and she looked incredibly pale. She slid off her clothes and examined her body. Surprisingly, there were no bruises or signs of trauma visible anywhere.

She opened her phone and sent a single text to her best friend.

I wrote you a letter. It's in my underwear drawer. Don't tell my parents.

She turned on the bathtub faucet and plugged the drain. Turning the handle all the way to the left, scalding hot water filled the tub. She sat down on the toilet and painfully relieved herself, blood staining the paper when she wiped. A few more tears rolled down her cheeks.

When the bathtub was about halfway full, she turned off the water. Gingerly, she retrieved her father's shaving kit, a little, black zippered pouch, from the cabinet under the sink. Unzipping it, she looked inside. It contained the usual shaving supplies: a little canister of shaving cream, a bottle of aftershave, and a straight razor. She removed the straight razor and turned it over in her hand. Her eyes locked onto the silver handle. A little pressure was all it took to release the stainless steel blade. She pressed her left thumb against the blade; it immediately bit into her skin. A droplet of blood slipped out of the cut and raced down her arm.

She lowered herself into the bathtub. She submerged herself to the neck in the near-boiling water, her skin turning bright red.

The tears flowed freely now.

"I'm sorry," she said.

She pressed the razor against her left arm; the blade dug deep into her skin. She gasped at the extreme pain of her skin splitting apart. Blood poured from the wound and swirled in the water. She dragged the knife up the length of her arm, stopping just below the bicep. She repeated the process on the other side. The wounds opened wide, turning her bath water into a dark red soup.

She released her grip on the razor and allowed it to sink to the bottom of the tub.

She leaned her head against the cool tile of the backsplash, tears racing down her face into the bloody pool of water.

She forced a smile, her one last act of defiance as the darkness overtook her.

Chapter 13

Everyone in the room was silent. Chase assumed everyone else was holding their breath, too, because he didn't hear them breathing. He released his breath slowly, allowing the air to escape from his barely open lips. He tried to make as little sound as possible, even avoiding shifting his weight from one foot to the other.

Floorboards creaked on the other side of the door, and the few slivers of light coming through the space at the bottom showed the shadows of two boots. The shadows grew bigger as the person approached the bedroom door. The sound of boots scuffing across the floor was impossibly loud in the otherwise silent room. Chase held the brass lamp he found on the bedside table like a baseball bat, causing his mind to drift back to Little League. How long had it been since he had held a bat? He exhaled again. He pictured them kicking the door open and rushing into the room, saw himself taking one, maybe two swings. He envisioned bashing one of the masked men in the head with those swings. It was something he did before football games. His dad called it visualizing success. Now he was visualizing survival. He squeezed the lamp even tighter. They probably couldn't take them all, but he was damn sure he was taking at least one of them with him.

Outside, the clouds shifted slightly. The faintest ray of moonlight passed through the windows. Chase could make out the silhouettes of his teammates, huddled in the center of the room with their weapons raised.

Someone tapped softly on the bedroom door.

Every muscle in his body tensed. He steeled his nerves, hoping he would have the courage to bash a man's skull when they entered the room. *Just take one with you*, he thought to himself.

Someone knocked again. This time, it was a playful knock, the same one that reminded Chase of his father. It echoed a rhythmic beat through the room.

Chase was acutely aware of the sweat beading down his chest and back, a single droplet sliding down the concave valley of his spine and rolling down his lower back. His white knuckles numbed as he tightened his grip against the brass lamp. The muscles in his shoulders started to shake under the weight.

Again that same playful knock.

Chase glanced to his left at Justin, his own fear was reflected in the older boy's eyes. Justin held the knife in his hand, the blade pointed down. Irish stood in front of him. Chase rested his left hand on Irish's shoulder, attempting to keep tabs on him in the darkness. Irish shook uncontrollably under his grip.

Behind him, Lemichael's breathing grew heavier. He sounded like he was hyperventilating. Stealing a quick glance back, Chase could see the red stains that blotched his face, evidence of the earlier beating.

"We got this," Chase whispered. Nobody responded, but Irish seemed to shake a little less.

Chase waited with anticipation for someone to kick the door in, sure the masked men would come flooding into the bedroom and hack them to bits with their machetes. Chase thought about his mom; he hoped the police wouldn't have her identify his mangled corpse. He didn't want her last memory of him to be some grotesque misrepresentation of who he was. That couldn't be the last memory of her baby boy.

The creaking of the floorboards on the other side of the bedroom door receded, accompanied by the heavy thudding of boots. He listened to the man's footsteps track down the hallway and into the living room. A light flutter filled Chase's chest; *Maybe they're leaving us alone*, he thought. The spark of hope gave him a renewed sense of resolve. He didn't move from his spot, not yet. The boys remained as rigid as statues and waited for the next sound.

After what felt like ten minutes, the sound of furniture legs scraping across the floor broke the silent standoff. The sound grew louder as the men pushed the furniture down the hallway.

A shift in the clouds blocked the moon, once again plummeting the room into darkness. There was a loud thud, and the door shook on its hinges. At the sound, the boys recoiled backward. They closed in on themselves, tightening their makeshift defensive circle.

"They're barricading us in," Irish whispered.

"Why would they do that?" Justin asked.

As if to answer his question, the window behind them shattered, a hailstorm of glass shards raining down on them. They jerked around, weapons raised. Through the darkness outside the broken window, they could see the faint outline of a man. The dark mesh covering the eyes gave him the appearance of a demon.

Before the boys could react, the window on the other side of the room exploded. A large chunk of glass caught Irish on the cheek. It drew a red line across his face, and a single droplet of blood seeped out.

"Get down," Justin shouted.

Almost in unison, the boys crouched.

"They're going to fucking shoot us," Lemichael wailed. His voice had lost any sense of confidence, reverting to a childish cry.

"Why haven't they done it yet?" Chase wondered aloud.

"Lemichael, watch the door. Everyone else, watch the windows," Justin commanded.

Chase jerked his attention back to the first window. He raised the brass lamp back up, prepared to swing at whoever was dumb enough to climb through. He strained his eyes against the darkness, watching shadows dart around outside the house. His eyes couldn't fixate on one silhouette against the darkness. Instead, their silhouettes mixed in with the trees behind them, giving the illusion of an army of masked attackers roaming about.

A metallic clicking noise pulled his attention toward the opposite window.

"What the fuck was that?" Justin said.

"I don't see anything!" Lemichael shouted.

Chase could make out a faint hissing noise. A subtle, sweet taste filled the air.

"What is that?" Justin shouted.

"I don't know, man. We gotta get out of here." Irish attempted to push past his teammates toward the door, but stopped. He bent over and began coughing. The hacks were so aggressive his eyes bulged and reddened.

Justin grabbed hold of the door handle and pulled. When it didn't open, he pulled harder. It didn't move. Justin turned around with a look of utter panic on his face. "We're locked in."

"What do we do?"

Chase couldn't tell who said it because he was beginning to feel lightheaded. His legs started to shake under his weight. Slowly, he lowered the lamp, unable to support its weight any longer.

Another minute passed in a panicked blur. Irish, continued his coughing fit and fell to one knee. He dropped his knife and slumped to the floor. Lemichael bent down, only to nearly collapse himself. He steadied himself against the bed's footboard and pressed his hand to Irish's chest to ensure he was still breathing.

"He's alive." The cadence of his speech was off, like someone with a thick southern drawl.

Chase felt the surrounding darkness swirling around him. He fought the urge to fall to his knees or close his eyes.

"We gotta get outta here," Justin slurred. Chase chuckled, losing himself in the drowsiness; it sounded like Justin was drunk.

What the hell did they give us that fucked us up in a couple minutes? Chase thought.

The knife slipped from Justin's hand and crashed to the floor. Chase reached for it but lost his balance and collapsed. He tried to sit up, but his muscles seemed too weak to support his weight. Somewhere above him, Justin beat against the door. Chase tried desperately to sit up one more time. His arms gave out, forcing him face-first against the cool wood floor. He laid there, listening to Justin throw himself repeatedly against the bedroom door. The thud of his body against the door grew weaker; his pleas to be let out grew fainter. Chase finally succumbed to the encroaching darkness.

Chapter 14

Dear Taylor,

I'm going to keep this short. You are the best friend I could've ever asked for. You've been there for me through thick and thin. That's why I wanted to make sure you know why I did it. I went to that party, the one you told me not to. Something really bad happened. I don't want to write the word, but I'm sure you can figure out what they did to me. I couldn't live with it.

Just know I love you. You're more than a best friend. You are my sister.

BBF...

P.S. Please don't tell my parents.

Taylor reread the note for what must have been the hundredth time. The black ink smeared across the page a little more with every tear she had cried for the last week. The smudges made the letter difficult to read, but it didn't matter. She had memorized every word. Just like they always did with their notes, she folded the letter in half, and then again until it was folded into a small square. Fearful someone might take it, she slid the letter into the most secure place she could think of: her bra.

Someone reached over and squeezed her hand. The contact startled her, causing her to shy away from it. The tough hand gripped harder, not willing to let her go. She looked down to see her own small, pale hand encompassed in one far larger than her own. Calluses marred the knuckles, worn from years of hard work. Her eyes traced over the hairy arm to her father's broad shoulders and scruffy face. His grip pulled her from her stupor. He refused to meet her eyes, but they glistened like she had never seen before. This was the closest she had ever come to seeing her father cry. She knew him to be the most stoic of men, who never talked about his feelings, and the realization shocked her. He kept his gaze fixed on the pastor. Taylor could tell he wasn't willing to risk looking down at her. He wouldn't risk letting the tears fall.

She knew he had seen her reading the letter and storing it away in her bra. He had asked her about it; she lied and told him it was the last note Kourtney had written her at school and she wanted to keep it close to her heart.

The shock was still fresh, and it turned the whole funeral into a blur. Her eyes drifted from the pastor to the black dress with a frilly back her mother had picked out for her. Taylor considered protesting, but knew she couldn't summon the strength to dress herself. For the first time in probably fifteen years, Taylor allowed her mom to dress her. She sat silently on a stool in her mother's bathroom while her mom sculpted her face with makeup. At the time, Taylor was sure the makeup would be wasted when she cried it away, but no tears came. A sense of numbness had taken hold of her. She regretted not speaking up about her mother's choice of dress sooner, because the straps criss crossed and scratched her shoulders every time she shifted in her seat. It was weird what her mind focused on when it should be grieving, almost like her subconscious was trying to distract her from the trauma.

The day Kourtney committed suicide, Taylor's phone buzzed. She had been too tired to get out of bed to check it. If she had, she would have seen the cryptic text message from Kourtney. She could have saved her best friend. Instead, she was here, preparing to bury the only person outside of her family she truly loved.

The night of the party, Taylor stayed up all night watching *The Shining* and *IT*; Kourtney loved Stephen King, even the movie adaptations. They planned to have a movie date at Taylor's house. Taylor purchased popcorn, ice cream, and a two-liter bottle of Sprite in preparation for their girls' night. There was a series of nail polish bottles on the nightstand waiting for one of Kourtney's exotic paint jobs. Taylor was beyond excited until Kourtney said she was going to a party at Hector Lopez's house. Their phone call quickly turned heated. Taylor begged Kourtney not to go; everyone knew those parties regularly got out of control. Every girl in school knew terrible things happened to girls when they hung out with the football team, and Taylor couldn't understand why the girls of Tall Oak continued to fall for their lies.

Taylor also knew Kourtney was determined to break through the "cool kid barrier," as they called it. The pair had joked for years about Kourtney pulling Taylor into the popular crowd. Taylor never had any interest in joining that club. She was content to get good grades, read horror books all night, and listen to nineties punk rock. A wave of heat rushed through her body. Why couldn't Kourtney have listened just this once? Why did she have to be so damn stubborn?

The pastor stood at the front of the church going on about God's plan and the tragedy of losing someone so young. He mentioned something about asking for help if you're struggling with depression. The words became gurgled static in her ears. She couldn't stand listening to this old man drone on about something he didn't understand.

Her father squeezed her hand tighter. She side-eyed him, trying to determine if the squeezing was for her benefit or his. A single tear broke the seal and rushed down his cheek. He pretended to scratch his chin with his free hand, wiping the tear away in the process. A part of her wanted to lean on her father, to squeeze his hand back, but the numb part of her couldn't summon the strength to act on it.

She looked across the aisle to where Mr. And Mrs. Rivers sat. Mr. Rivers sat straight up. His face was blank and unreadable; his demeanor seemed detached. Mrs. Rivers sobbed hysterically. Her cries drowned out the pastor's never-ending speech. She stared at the couple who had been like a second set of parents to her for most of her life. They didn't look like the same people she had come to love. They looked broken. Taylor hoped her own parents wouldn't look like that at her funeral.

Taylor peeked over her shoulder at the crowd behind her; most of the town was in attendance. She imagined most of these people felt obligated to attend a teenager's funeral, especially in a town as small as Tall Oak. Things like this didn't happen in quiet little Christian communities. She pictured the old bats at the hair salon talking poorly about the Rivers family, but in their not-so-subtle southern charm. She could hear them already. "Bless her heart, but that Mrs. Rivers must not have taught little Kourtney right from wrong." The sight of these people pretending to weep for a girl they never knew sickened her. That sickening feeling only grew worse when she glimpsed Ford's gigantic frame hunched over in a pew near the back. It looked like he was speaking to someone. Taylor rocked to her right and craned her neck to get a view around the sea of people. He was talking to Justin Jackson, and Justin was laughing. A streak of ice ran through her veins; he was getting away with it and laughing about it.

The funeral services dragged on for what seemed like an eternity. Taylor sat patiently, glancing back every few minutes at the football players in the back of the room. She caught glances of Irish, Hector, Lemichael, and Nick through the crowd. They seemed to be passing around a phone. They took turns examining something on the screen and laughing before they passed it to the next person. When the service ended, Taylor gave the obligatory hugs and listened to people tell her Kourtney was in a better place. It took about an hour to get through all of that, but to the grief-stricken Taylor, it was a few minutes of fake gestures and empty words.

Once nearly everyone left, she allowed herself to approach her best friend's casket. The funeral home dressed Kourtney in a purple dress, with a bow in her hair. It made her look even younger than her short seventeen years; Kourtney would have hated it. Taylor removed a ring from her middle finger and turned it over in her palm. Engraved on the inside were the letters "BBF." She gently took one of Kourtney's icy fingers and slid the ring on it. She smiled at the memory of the two of them at the mall getting their friendship rings engraved. Kourtney had been so afraid of her parents finding out what the engraving meant. After several minutes, Taylor finally convinced her to lie to them. They agreed that to anyone else, "BBF" stood for best buds forever. Taylor wiped away a tear and whispered, "Best Bitch Forever."

Later that night, Taylor leaned against the headboard of her bed reading Kourtney's letter over and over again. She traced every word with her finger, examined the curves of the lettering, took it all in.

She became frustrated as she waited for her parents to go into their room and close their door. Finally, with her eyes weakened from the strain of reading in the dark, her parents went to bed. She gave it about an hour to be sure they were asleep before she slid out of her bed. Careful to avoid the springs she knew would generate the most noise, she lowered herself to the floor and tiptoed into the hallway. She made her way into the bathroom and pulled open the mirror that doubled as a medicine cabinet. A bottle of antidepressants her mother's psychiatrist prescribed to Taylor stood prominently on the shelf. The doctor told her mother the pills would help Taylor get through this difficult time, at least until she managed to cope with her best friend's death. If only the doctor knew how right he was. She emptied the pill bottle into her pocket so it wouldn't sound like a maraca when she walked. She grabbed a water bottle from the kitchen and slipped out the front door, carefully closing it behind her.

There was a playground about halfway between her house and Kourtney's house. The two would meet there every day after school when they were kids. They would play until the streetlights came on, then sprint back to their respective homes. The big tower in the center of the playground, with its different color slides coming out of it, was their castle. They pretended to be princesses and took turns rescuing each other from a make-believe dragon. When they were older, they sat at the top and talked about the boys they liked. This year, they spent their nights sitting at the top and planning their futures together. It was in this very spot they decided they would go to Florida State together. It was close to Tall Oak, and they could be roommates. They both wanted to major in business: Taylor in Marketing, Kourtney in Project Management. After graduation, they would move out west to start a business together.

That was their plan, anyway, for the two of them to never be apart.

Now, Taylor sat at the top of their castle alone. Kourtney wasn't here to save her from the dragon terrorizing her mind. She reclined in her usual spot next to the purple slide. She unscrewed the cap on her bottle of water and gulped down a mouthful. Her mouth was painfully dry despite the water. She dug her hand into her pocket and removed the handful of pills. One by one, she popped them into her mouth and washed them down.

She sunk a little lower and pulled Kourtney's letter from her bra. The little square was already showing signs of wear and tear from the constant use. Quickly unfolding the letter, she re-read it one more time. When she was done, she laid the letter neatly on the floor. She removed her shoe and used it as a paperweight. She might not be able to tell Kourtney's parents, but the police could when they found the letter.

After a while, extreme drowsiness set in. Taylor struggled to hold her eyes open and shivered despite the warm, humid Florida night. Her fingers caressed the letter.

She smiled.

They might not be able to go to college or fight imaginary dragons anymore, but they would still be together.

Chapter 15

Chase awoke to shouting. The words hit his ears and lost form in his mind. He desperately tried to open his eyes, but they seemed glued together. On instinct, he tried to raise his hands to his eyes, but they were stuck.

The screamed words took shape.

"Do you know who my fucking father is? Do you? You dumb fucks made a huge mistake. I'll tell you what, you let us go, and I'll tell my dad to go easy on you."

It was Justin's voice, and he was screaming at their attackers. Adrenaline flooded Chase's veins. He raised his eyebrows as high as he could and peeled his eyelids open. The obscenely bright lights blinded him to the scene.

Justin continued to scream. "You guys fucked up big time. You should let us go right now and save yourselves a lot of trouble."

Chase jerked his head toward his friend's voice. The scene before him shifted from blinding light to blurry shapes, and finally into a properly formed picture. In that last moment, when his eyes finally adjusted to the light, he realized their precarious position.

Thick, gray duct tape wrapped around his wrists and cemented them to armrests. His fingers swelled under the pressure, a faint hint of purple coloring the tips. Tape ran down the entire length of his calves, pinching the muscles against chair legs. Only his head remained unrestrained, allowing him to look around and take in his surroundings.

To his left, Justin continued yelling. Tape wrapped around his body, making him one with his chair. The tape dug into his skin. The circulation was cutting off at the wrists and ankles; his hands and feet were even more swollen and discolored than Chase's.

Irish and Lemichael were beside Justin, each taped to their own personal prison. The wounds on Lemichael's face from the beating Chase had put on him earlier had reopened. A river of blood flooded from his nose and mixed with the blood seeping from his lips. He appeared to be on the verge of unconsciousness. Chase wondered if something had happened to Lemichael while the group was unconscious. Looking at Irish, Chase noticed the boy wasn't screaming like Justin; he simply clenched his eyelids together. A single tear escaped and made its way down his cheek before getting lost in the boy's stubble.

Chase shifted his head around. It felt heavy on his neck, and he imagined he looked drunk as he repositioned his face to the scene in front of him. The rush of adrenaline he had built up drained from his body, quickly replaced with ice water. His heart stopped beating momentarily, and he choked on his saliva. Five masked men stood in front of them.

They were each painted in blood. The crimson liquid stained their clothes and drained from their boots. Four of them stood scattered around the room. One leaned against the wall next to the TV with a machete dangling from his fingertips. Another sat on the edge of the recliner, elbows on his knees, hands propping up his head, his machete resting against the chair. A man wearing the bloodiest outfit squatted in the corner. The fourth man was standing behind the last, offset slightly. The fifth man stood close to the boys, his head cocked to the right. He swung his machete back and forth at his side.

"They're all awake," a voice from his right said. Chase jerked his head in that direction. The violent wrench of his neck caused the vertebrae at the base of his skull to pop. A sixth masked man was sitting on one of Justin's coolers. The tip of his machete dug into the wood planks of the floor. He spun it with his right hand, leaving deep scratches with each rotation.

"Let's get started," another voice said. Chase couldn't see this man but could tell the voice was coming from over his left shoulder. A pair of gloved hands gripped his shoulders and squeezed. A bolt of pain shot through his traps and radiated up his neck.

"Are you ready, Chase?"

A seventh rabbit. This one sounded familiar to him. He couldn't place it, though. Craning his neck, more gently this time, he tried to look over his right shoulder but couldn't see the man's face, which he knew was pointless. He was sure the man wore a mask like the others.

The man standing in front of the group stopped swinging his blade back and forth. Slowly, he lifted the machete and grabbed it by the back of the blade, passing it to the man behind him. He squatted down in front of the boys and stared at them through the eyeholes of his plastic rabbit mask. Dried blood and viscera stuck to the rabbit ears and stained the white parts. He raised his hands and slid the mask off, revealing his face. His black hair curled at the ends and hung in an unkempt mess around his face. His blue eyes stared at Justin, giving the impression he was looking through the boy. Chase could see hatred boiling up behind those eyes.

One of the other rabbits spoke up. "I thought we were keeping our masks on man?" Chase detected the sound of a Southern accent but didn't recognize the voice.

The man rubbed the stubble on his chin. "No point now. We're going through with this." He reached forward and tapped Justin on his leg.

"Do you know who I am?" His voice was flat and emotionless.

Justin shook his head. The man stood up and looked down at Justin. He raised his arm and backhanded Justin across the face, igniting it in a burning red. The indents of the man's knuckles burrowed deep into his cheeks.

"You speak when you're spoken to. Do you know who I am?" The monotone voice was replaced by a vicious growl.

"No," Justin snarled.

The man raised his other hand and backhanded Justin on the other side of his face. His bottom lip ripped open, and a squirt of blood struck Chase's face.

"Hey! Leave him alone!" Irish shouted. One of the men behind them laughed as the sound of his stomping boots carried him closer.

The man turned his head toward Irish. "I wasn't speaking to you, fire crotch." He spat the insult out with disgust.

The man standing behind the boys swung a belt around Irish's throat and cinched it tight. Irish's mouth flew open as he fought for air. Veins throbbed in his temples and face turned purple at an alarming rate. Irish's eyes bulged as his fingers trembled against the armrest.

The first man turned back to Justin. "Where are your manners? You should call me sir." The man's voice carried a mocking tone.

"Sir, sir! Please! You're going to kill him!" Justin shouted.

The man waved a hand, and the person choking Irish released him. Irish jerked forward as much as his restraints would allow, gasping and coughing. The purple slowly retreated from his face. He slumped back and sucked in deep, exaggerated breaths.

"See, that wasn't so hard, was it?" the man asked as he winked at Justin.

Justin shook his head. "No, sir." The defeat in the team captain's voice caused Chase's pulse to quicken even more. The boy never got rattled, never defeated.

The man smiled. "So I guess it's time we introduce ourselves and explain why we're here. What do you think?"

"Yes, sir," Justin stammered.

The assailant stuck his outstretched hand toward the man sitting in the recliner, who slapped the TV remote in the unmasked man's hand. Turning his back on the confined boys, he turned on the TV. Justin must have left his laptop plugged in, because his home screen burst to life on the flatscreen. The man navigated to the video player from his spot in the recliner. The screen went dark, a white play button in the middle. It was the video of Chase sleeping with his girlfriend, the last thing the boys watched before going to sleep.

The man, who seemed to be their leader, walked over to the open laptop and minimized the video. He looked over his shoulder. "Don't worry, Chase, we'll come back to that one."

He clicked on PowerPoint, revealing some nude girl sprawled across Nick's bed. The man scrolled through the slides until he reached the one he was looking for. The picture was of Kourtney Rivers, clearly passed out on Hector's bed. She was completely naked, her legs spread open to reveal her swollen and bruised groin. The unmasked man shook his head and made a clicking sound with his tongue.

Justin and Lemichael shared a glance. They tried to catch Irish's eyes, but he was fighting to remain conscious. A thin, purple bruise formed around Irish's neck, circling him like a scarf.

The man turned back to the four boys taped to their chairs, tears freely flowing down his face. "A father should never have to see his daughter like that." He threw a thumb behind him in the direction of the screen. Chase noticed the other masked men looked away from the screen. Some were looking at the tied-up boys; most were looking at their feet. They were either uncomfortable at the appearance of the naked girl on the screen or trying to show respect to the daughter of their accomplice.

"My name," the man continued as he wiped the tears from his face, "is Jack Rivers." He squatted down in front of the boys again. "And that is," he paused to correct himself, "was my daughter." He stood up and walked over to Lemichael. "I heard you knew my daughter pretty well; maybe too well?"

Lemichael shook his head, his eyes swimming with fear. Jack twisted his mouth into an exaggerated frown. "Didn't you learn anything from your buddy over there?" He smashed his fist into Lemichael's face, sending the chair tumbling backward. A thunderous crack rang out from the broken bones in Lemichael's nose. The man who choked Irish caught the chair before it fell. Jack shook his hand. "You speak when spoken to," he shouted.

Lemichael's nose was flattened against his face. Blood ejected from his wound and puddled onto the floor. Lemichael made a wet, wheezing noise as he swallowed his own blood. He retched violently, spitting the blood out of his mouth. Chase watched the red liquid consume his friend and drench the front of his shirt.

Jack continued to shake his hand out and turned away from Lemichael. He paced in front of them, the floorboards creaking under his weight. "Now, you boys have gotten away with some fucked up shit for quite some time, your daddies always protecting you and brushing your sick little games under the rug. Well, me and my friends," he paused and spun around with his arms outstretched, "we're not going to stand for it anymore. You little cunts took something from each of us, and now you're going to pay for it." He stopped pacing and held out his hand. The man leaning against the wall pushed himself upright, stepped forward, and slid something into Jack's outstretched hand. It was impossible to see what the item was from Chase's position.

Jack walked back to Lemichael and knelt down in front of him. Flashing a wicked smile, he brandished a small handheld hedge clipper. He snapped closed the handle twice; the blades made a swishing noise as they came together and separated. Lemichael thrashed in his chair. "No, no, no, please! Don't do this. I'm sorry! I'm sorry! Don't." Lemichael's cries were deafening. Jack grabbed hold of Lemichael's right thumb and forced it between the blades of the hedge clipper.

"I want to hear you tell me what you did to my daughter." The determination in his voice convinced the entire room he was serious.

"I didn't do shit to her, man!" Lemichael's pleading turned to sobs.

"If you lie again, I take something more precious from you," Jack said with a wink.

"Ok, we did it, man. Don't do this."

Jack's face twisted into a look of impatience. "Say it, you perverted little fuck!"

"We raped her!"

Utter silence met the announcement. Even Lemichael's cries seemed stifled.

Jack nodded and waved his hand at the other boys. "All of them?"

Lemichael spat blood away from his mouth. His nose still gushed all over. "Yes, sir. Well, all of us except Chase. He didn't go to the party."

Jack nodded again. "Did Chase assault any of the girls in this slide show?"

Lemichael vigorously shook his head. "No, sir, there is a video of him, but I think it was consensual."

"Did he know they were being recorded?"

Justin spoke up this time. "No, sir. I put a camera in the room. He had no idea. Please don't hurt him!"

Jack looked up at the man standing behind the boys. "See Zach? I told you Megan and Chase didn't know the video was being made."

Chase finally realized why he recognized the voice behind him. It was his girlfriend's dad.

"Never doubted you, Chase," Zach Connolly said from somewhere behind him. Chase bowed his head, realizing the situation was even worse than he initially realized. These men knew them, and obviously, each had their own vendetta against the boys. He tried to piece together who the other men were, but it turned out he didn't need to.

"Alright, it's time to get this party started," Jack said. "I'm going to finish introducing myself, and then my friends are going to come around and introduce themselves." With that, he squeezed the grips of the hedge clippers together. An ear-shattering crack filled the room, and the clippers broke through the bone in Lemichael's thumb. For a moment, Lemichael didn't scream. His eyes widened, mouth stretching as if to scream, but no noise escaped. The thumb bounced off the floor, and a shot of blood spurted from the severed stub. Lemichael finally released a groan and followed it up with a shriek.

Jack stood up and passed the clippers to another man. Jack stepped away from the boys, sliding his rabbit mask back onto his face. From the way the mask lifted on his face, Chase could tell that Jack was smiling.

Justin vomited on himself, coating the front of his shirt in bile.

Chase lowered his head and did the only thing he could think to do in that horrible moment. He prayed.

Chapter 16

"I'm so sorry for your loss, Ronald," the pastor said as he exited the room. Ron winced; he hated being called Ronald. Ronald Hill Sr. named his only son after himself. Most people would consider this an act of love, but it was just another selfish act in a long line of crippling narcissism for his father. After nearly thirty years, the sound of his own name brought him back to those beatings.

Ron closed the door behind the pastor and watched through the window as the old man got into his Toyota Camry. He caught himself wondering how the nineties shit box was still running. Tape held the front bumper together, and a spider-web-like crack adorned the windshield. He lingered at the window a moment longer, watching the Camry blow white smoke from its exhaust.

He turned back to his living room. His wife rested in a near catatonic state on the couch. She refused to allow anyone to help her with her hair, instead electing to leave it half combed this morning. The ordinarily elegant brown hair gave off the appearance of a rat's nest on her head. Ron had been the one to dress her this morning. He chose the same black dress she had worn for her mother's funeral; she refused to help him, lying motionless on the bed while he shimmied the dress onto her petite frame. It seemed appropriate to put her in heels for an occasion like this, but he had the good sense to put her in a pair of black flats. She kicked those off the moment they returned from the funeral, immediately collapsing on the couch, her dress wrinkled into a disheveled mess of cloth. Ron desperately searched his wife's blue eyes for any sign of life, but the fire he'd fallen in love with was extinguished. Taylor's death broke her.

Ron looked about the house. Casserole dishes lined the table. Their guests left dirty cups and plates stacked on end tables. What was the point of these people coming over to "help" if they were just going to leave a mess?

The last people there were Jack and Roxanne, Kourtney's parents. Despite losing their daughter only a week prior, they were in much better shape than Ron and his wife. Ron could hear the water turn on in the kitchen, followed by the familiar clanking of dishes being loaded into the dishwasher.

Ron was grateful for their help. He wasn't sure if it was because the burden of losing a child united them or if it was simply because they were friends, but they were the only people Ron wanted around. He was tired of everyone repeating the same tired, old lines. At least his friends had the good decency not to say much.

Ron watched as Jack gathered dishes from around the house and carried them into the kitchen, depositing them on the countertop for his wife to wash. He re-emerged from the kitchen with a trash bag. Ron watched Jack walk around the living and dining rooms, scooping up trash. When Jack shoved the last of the trash into the bag, he tied it into a knot and moved to the back door.

"Hey, Jack, why don't I give you a hand with that?" Ron asked.

"That's alright, buddy. I think I can manage."

"Roxi will sit with her for a minute. Rox, can you come sit with Heather for a minute?" Ron insisted. Jack shot him a suspicious look, but Ron shook his head in silent reply.

The sound of running water stopped, and Roxanne appeared in the living room. "Of course," Roxanne said through a smile. Ron could tell the smile seemed genuine, but her eyes seemed void of happiness. He wondered if his wife would carry those same dead eyes.

Ron walked around the edge of the couch and followed Jack outside. The sun was dipping below the trees that lined his back fence. The moisture in the air clung to his clothes, and sweat immediately pooled under his arms. Jack led them around the side of the house to where the outdoor trash cans waited. He removed the lid and tossed the bag inside. Jack gagged at the smell of rotting garbage, hurriedly slamming the lid back down.

"I forgot to take the trash to the curb," Ron explained.

Jack nodded and patted Ron on the shoulder. "I'm really sorry about all this, man. I hated when people told me they knew what I was going through, but in your case, I really do." Jack squeezed his friend's shoulder.

Ron fished a folded-up piece of paper from his back pocket.

"I have to talk to you about something, Jack. It's going to be real hard to hear, but I wanted you to know." He unfolded the letter, more for Jack's sake than for his own. He already memorized every letter. "I think this letter explains the death of both of our girls."

Tears welled up in Jack's eyes. The ordinarily stoic man looked smaller than usual. It reminded Ron of how his friend looked during Kourtney's funeral. Ron couldn't help but wonder if he looked like that now.

"I didn't want the women to know, not yet, but I have to tell you." Ron shifted his weight back and forth on his feet.

Jack squeezed Ron's shoulder then crossed his arms over his chest. "OK?" His voice dripped with trepidation.

Ron inhaled deeply. He had so much confidence when he decided to tell Jack about Kourtney's suicide note. That sense of confidence was eluding him now. He felt like a child, afraid to show his dad a poor report card. He pushed through the discomfort and cleared his throat.

"So you know, I was the one that found Taylor's," he swallowed the sob building in his throat, "body." Jack nodded. Ron could see the man physically preparing himself for the bad news.

"I found a suicide note," he continued.

Jack's mouth fell open. He uncrossed his arms and stepped forward. "I thought Taylor didn't leave a note?"

This was the part Ron had been dreading. He looked down at his feet, unable to meet his friend's eyes. "It wasn't Taylor's." The air around them felt heavy. Ron prayed Jack would get the reference and he wouldn't have to spell it out.

"Was it from Kourtney?"

Ron nodded his head slowly. He kept his eyes locked on his shoelaces.

"What did it say? Let me read it?" His words came out in an exasperated plea.

"I'm not sure you want to; it's pretty hard to read."

Jack snatched it from his hand. He read the few short lines Kourtney had left for her best friend, the few lines Ron knew led to Taylor's own death.

"I don't understand. What does it mean? What party?"

Now it was Ron's turn to place a hand on his friend's shoulder. He raised his head and locked eyes with Jack. He knew he had just peeled off the scab that had formed on Jack's heart over the last couple of weeks.

"The night before Kourtney's death, she was supposed to come over here. Do you remember?"

Jack nodded.

"She never came over. Taylor told me she wasn't feeling well. I thought nothin' of it at the time; teenagers change plans, ya know? But this letter says that she went to a party instead. I asked some of Taylor's friends, and Hector Lopez threw a party that night."

Jack's expression was blank. Ron wasn't sure the man was comprehending his words. An awkward silence fell over them. Ron tried to wait patiently for the words to click. When Jack didn't indicate he understood, Ron resigned himself to saying it out loud.

"I think those boys hurt her," Ron finally blurted out.

Jack stepped away from his friend. He wobbled and looked as if he was about to collapse. Ron reached out to steady him, locking an arm under Jack's shoulder to support him.

"We have to go to the police," Jack whispered. Jack felt like he couldn't breathe in enough oxygen to speak in a normal tone. His chest constricted at the thought of his baby girls being hurt by those boys.

Ron nodded. "That's what I wanted to do as well, but I'm worried about Hector's dad being a cop."

Jack sucked in a deep breath. He stood upright, waving a hand dismissively. "I'm good now."

"I made copies," Ron said. "I have a feeling this isn't going to go well."

Jack's hands were trembling. "What do we tell our wives?" he asked.

"Nothing. My wife can't handle this right now. We have Rox stay with Heather, and we handle this."

Jack nodded his agreement.

The two men rushed inside, gathering their wallets, phones, and keys, hustling out the front door without telling their wives where they were going. Filled with determination, Jack slammed his car door so hard it rocked the vehicle. The tires squealed when he smashed his foot against the accelerator. He exceeded the speed limit by at least twenty-five miles per hour, but Ron noticed his friend slowed down as they approached the police department's headquarters. A few roads away, he reduced his speed to twenty over, then fifteen, then ten. Ron hoped Jack wasn't losing his nerve. He wasn't sure he could do this alone.

They pulled into a visitor parking space near the front of the station, and Ron led them inside. The man sitting at the desk did not look very inviting. His face contained deep creases from years of stress. He didn't bother to acknowledge the two men as they approached.

Jack cleared his throat, but the man continued typing on his computer. Jack cleared his throat again, this time much louder. The man slammed his finger against the enter key and looked up. "How can I help you?" he asked in a monotone voice that screamed of disinterest.

"We, uh, we need to report a crime," Ron stammered.

"What kind of crime?"

Ron looked at Jack. "We don't really know."

The man behind the desk grunted and told them to follow him. He walked out from behind his desk and led them down a corridor and into a room.

"An officer will be with you shortly," he said.

Just before the man closed the door, Jack caught it. "Oh, and can you make sure it's not Officer Lopez or the chief?" Jack asked.

The man gave him a puzzled look before pulling the door shut. Jack and Ron took seats on one side of the table and waited for an officer to come in. The walls were off-white, and Ron wasn't sure if they had been painted that way or had faded from years of neglect. The room was empty except for a metal table bolted to the floor and four metal folding chairs.

The door swung open, and another tired-looking man entered the room. This man was not in the standard khaki uniform of the Tall Oak Police Department. Instead, he wore slacks with a white shirt tucked into his belt. He swung his black coat off and draped it around the back of the chair. Ron and Jack jumped to their feet and stuck out their hands. The officer slumped into his chair without shaking.

"Have a seat," he said. Ron and Jack exchanged a confused look before returning to their chairs.

"I don't have much time, so why don't you gentlemen tell me why you're here?"

Ron spoke first. "Well, we think a crime occurred."

"You think?" the officer snapped.

"We have some evidence," Jack interjected. He pulled the note from his pocket and passed it to the officer. The officer unfolded it and read over it.

"It doesn't say who or what happened."

"Yes, sir, but we know that she was at a party that night. We know that something happened that led to my daughter committing suicide," Jack said.

The officer shook his head. "Ok, whose party was it?" Ron and Jack exchanged a glance.

"Hector Lopez," Ron said.

The officer stared at him. He bit his bottom lip. "You mean Deputy Lopez's son?"

Ron nodded. "Yes."

"And we think Lemichael and Nick Sanders were involved," Jack offered.

The officer snapped his head in Jack's direction. "The chief's sons?"

Jack nodded. "Yes, sir, that's why we didn't want to report it directly to them."

The officer rubbed his five o'clock shadow while he studied the letter. He glanced up at the men and then back down at the paper. Without warning, he stood up and ripped the door open.

"Stay here," he said, slamming the door behind him.

"I fucking knew it," Ron said.

Jack shook his head. "You think he's going to tell the chief?"

"Guess we will see in a minute. Good thing I made those copies."

A few moments later, the door flew open, and Chief Sanders marched in, dropped into the chair the previous officer had been sitting in. He leaned back with his legs spread apart, reeking of cockiness. Ron vaguely remembered him from high school. The two didn't run in the same crowd, but Sanders had been a star athlete, and everyone knew him.

"So, I hear you two want to accuse my boys of a crime," the chief said.

"We said they might have been involved," Ron replied.

"Yeah, we asked around, and they were at a party. My daughter was at that party, and we think some of the football players did something to her," Jack said, his voice growing more agitated.

The chief shot him a look that would make Medusa jealous. He picked up the letter and read it. Ron bounced his legs. If his wife had been here, she would have reminded him his nervous habit was unprofessional and that he should learn to control it.

"Those boys didn't do nothing. Those are good boys. They're all going off to college next year, and we're not about to have y'all drag them through the mud." The chief's eyes burned with rage. He was leaning forward in his seat now, his posture a little more rigid.

"Chief, you have to look into this!" Jack shouted.

The chief jumped to his feet. His chair fell away from him and crashed to the floor. He pointed a finger at Jack's face. "You listen here, you little bitch; nobody is going to hear a word about this." He shifted his weight and stuck his finger in Ron's face. "I will not have you spreading vicious lies about my sons or those boys." He stood upright. "If I hear so much as a fucking whisper about this again, I will ruin your fucking lives."

Jack jumped to his feet and slammed his fists into the table. "Your fucked up little sons already did that. Come on, Ron." The anger in Jack's voice shocked Ron. As mad as he was, there was a level of coldness to Jack's voice. A subtle inflection in the words made Ron's heart skip a beat.

Ron rose to his feet. He leaned over the table so he was eye to eye with the chief. "This isn't over."

The chief pointed to the door. "Get out of my station."

"Gladly," Jack snapped.

Ron paused at the door. "Any chance I can get that letter back?"

The chief folded his arms over his chest. A smirk stretched across his face. "What letter?"

"Thought so. What a fucking asshole," Ron said as he shuffled out of the room with Jack on his heels. The two men retreated from the building and loaded themselves into Jack's Jeep. They watched as the chief exited the building and stood in front of the exit with his arms crossed, that same smirk on his face. As Jack put the truck into reverse and backed out of the parking space, the chief gave a sarcastic wave.

"We're going to make him regret this," Jack said. Ron glared at his friend's face. The typically friendly dentist was no longer there, now replaced with a being of pure hatred.

Chapter 17

"Whoa, what the fuck!" Chase screamed. He thrashed against the tape holding him in place but was unable to tear free.

Beside him, Justin stammered a series of incoherent protests. His face flushed a bright red. Irish's head bobbed up and down with each breath, battling a panic attack and the hyperventilating that comes with it.

Chase expected Lemichael to pass out from the pain, but he remained fully conscious. His shriek was a sound unlike anything Chase had ever heard before. It was an animalistic howl. The sound was so high-pitched that Chase would have covered his ears if he could have.

Another masked man stepped up. He slid his rabbit mask up so it rested atop his head. His face was incredibly ordinary. Chase saw no major distinguishing features. He was clean-shaven, not fat but not skinny. He grabbed Lemichael's pointer finger and slid the hedge clippers over it.

"My name is George Davis. You little pricks have tormented my daughter Natalie for years. A nude photo got sent around the school this year. I'm not sure which of you did it, but I do know it was one of you." Tears welled up in George's eyes. "My mother saw those photos." His voice was trembling now. "She hasn't talked to Natalie since then." He looked back at Lemichael and locked eyes with him. Lemichael's eyes were wild, like a trapped animal on some nature documentary. They met George's gaze before darting down to the hedge clippers wrapped around his finger.

"I'm sorry!" Lemichael screamed.

George shook his head. "I knew it." Chase saw the muscles in George's arm tighten, and he looked away right as the clippers dug into his friend's finger. Lemichael squealed this time. The same sickening crack filled the room again as the clippers broke through the bone. Chase looked back to see George Davis holding Lemichael's severed pointer finger in his hand. He wiggled it in front of Lemichael's face in a "no, no" gesture. A streak of blood spurted from the nub where the finger used to be. George flicked the severed finger into Lemichael's face. It slapped into him with a wet thud before tumbling into his lap, leaving a streak of blood running from under his right eye to his lips.

Chase noticed most of the masked men were lining up now. He couldn't seem to grasp the reality of it all. How could these men be so cold? How could they be so eager? Their blood-stained jumpsuits and the smears of bodily fluids on their previously white rabbit masks offered no answers. Beside him, Justin continued to scream. He was pleading with the men to stop. His cries went through a cycle of begging, threatening, and hysterical sobs. Irish must have woken up, because his cries now intermingled with the cries of his other two remaining teammates. Chase didn't bother begging. He didn't bother crying. These men had already taken it too far; it wouldn't stop now. The realization sucked the breath from his chest.

I'm going to die here, he thought to himself.

Chase closed his eyes and prayed. At first, it was a silent prayer in his head, but as another man stepped up to Lemichael and introduced himself as Austin Thomas, his prayers escalated into fevered whispers.

"Your buddy Ford raped my daughter," Austin Thomas said. "I already made him pay. I would say that makes us even." Chase refused to look at the scene unfolding before him. He heard the sound of the blades on the hedge clippers sliding past each other several times. "But, you pigs deserve this."

Another sickening crack pierced Chase's eardrums. He squeezed his eyes tighter and allowed his praying to grow a little louder. Justin, Irish, and Lemichael continued their pleas to end the torture. Their loud shouts drowned out the sounds of Chase's prayers.

"I'm Mikeis Winston," another voice said. Another sickening crack followed the introduction. Again another man stepped forward and introduced himself. Again a sickening crack and deafening wails followed the introduction. Chase begged for Lemichael to pass out, but he didn't. This grotesque series of introductions continued until six of the seven men introduced themselves and took their pound of flesh.

Chase opened his eyes when the seventh man didn't step forward. The last man stood in the corner of the room, far away from the restrained boys. His gaze fixed upon Chase. The man ignored the previous dad, Kyle Simpson, as he held out the hedge clippers, simply shaking his head.

The voice Chase recognized as belonging to Jack Rivers spoke up from behind his mask. "We all have to participate. That ensures nobody can snitch on the others," Jack said. He snatched the clippers from Kyle and held them out to Zach. "That was the deal."

"I know," Zach Connolly answered. "And I'll do my part when the time comes."

Jack paused and tilted his head. His mask obscured his face, but Chase imagined the man's twisted expression. The confidence in Zach's voice must have put him at ease, though. After a pause, he nodded and pointed at another of the masked men. "Did you get the stove going?"

The man nodded. "Sure did."

"Ok, go get me the blade. We need to cauterize these wounds before Lemichael bleeds out." He reached out and patted Lemichael on the cheek. Lemichael's head lulled lazily to one side. He was still conscious, but shock and blood loss were clearly taking a toll.

The man left the room and walked toward the kitchen.

Chase took this lull in activity to examine his friend. Lemichael's eyes were glossed over. Their attackers had removed all five fingers from his right hand, an uneven series of bloody stumps protruding from his blood-soaked hand. Most of the fingers were cut behind the first knuckle, leaving as little finger material as possible. His thumb was missing from his left hand. The severed fingers lay scattered across the floor, a pool of blood around them. It grew larger with each passing second as more and more of it seeped from the wounds and flowed down the chair.

The man reappeared from the kitchen, carrying a large butcher knife which he handed to Jack. The knife blade glowed bright red. Chase cringed at the sight of it and the anticipation of what was about to come. Jack leaned forward and pressed the blade against the stump where Lemichael's thumb used to be. The flesh sizzled as it burned, sending out the stench of cooked skin mixed with a coppery smell of blood that assaulted Chase's nose. Lemichael gasped, but the sudden sucking in of air ended as abruptly as it had begun. Lemichael's head finally slumped forward, and the boy lost consciousness. Jack continued pressing the burning blade against each wound. The sizzle repeated itself, and the malodor grew stronger. Irish, who was sitting closest to Lemichael, retched. Vomit erupted and coated the floor in front of him in bile.

One of the men gagged from behind his rabbit mask. "Shit, I'm going to be sick," he said as he fled from the room. The man threw open the front door and vomited on the front porch. The splash of vomit hitting the porch almost sent Chase over the edge as he struggled to hold back the contents of his own stomach.

Jack lifted his mask when the man returned from the front porch. "You good?"

"Yeah, just hate throw up," the man replied. One of the masked men in the back released a little chuckle. Jack glanced back, and the chuckles stopped.

"Put the flash drive in," Jack ordered. One of the masked men stepped forward and slid a flash drive into the computer. The man pressed a few keys, and a slide show popped up on the TV. It began running through various pictures of little girls. Some of them showed the girls fishing, swimming, or riding their bikes. As the slide show progressed, the girls grew older. The pictures became the first day of high school photos, the first homecoming dance, and acceptance to college. The last picture of two beautiful girls smiling while throwing up a "peace" sign flashed across the screen and faded from view. Jack turned back toward the boys. Tears flowed freely down his face. He pointed a finger at the blank screen.

"Those are our little girls. A father is supposed to protect his daughters. He is supposed to teach them right from wrong, how to be a good person, and how to know which boys to trust." He released a little sniffle as he struggled to compose himself. "In that endeavor, every man in this room failed. We failed because we couldn't protect them from the monsters, from you." He waved the knife across the boys. "Me and Ron here," another man stepped forward and removed his mask, "we will never get to walk our daughters down the aisle at their weddings or hold our grandchildren." Ron was crying now too. "You took that from us. You took everything from us. We couldn't protect them from you, but we can protect the rest of them."

"Is the water boiling?" Jack asked in a menacing tone.

"Sure is," one of the masked men answered. Chase's skin broke out in goosebumps as the realization of what those words could mean set in. He stared at Justin. Justin was pale, the color retreating from his face.

Jack walked across the room and snatched Justin by the hair. He forced his head back and stared into Justin's eyes.

"That water is for you." Jack smiled. "And yes, it's going to hurt."

Chapter 18

Kyle Simpson leaned back in his chair, pushing the front two legs off the ground. His folded arms hid the Kiss logo on the front of his shirt. He shook his head back and forth, and his lips pressed together.

"No, that won't work," he said after a moment of silence.

"Well, why not?" George Davis asked.

"Because the son of a bitch is best friends with the commissioner of the FDLE," Kyle replied.

Austin Thomas nodded. "It's true. I've seen Chief Sanders at the golf course with this tall, blonde guy. I'm pretty sure he's in charge of the FDLE. Saw him with a bunch of cops the other day, cuttin' up."

Kyle unfolded his arms and threw his hand in Austin's direction. "See, we can't go to the state police because they're all buddies. As soon as we mention the Sanders brothers, that pussy with the FDLE will call up the chief, and he'll fuck our lives up. It's a good ole boy network, and we ain't part of it," he said with audible disdain.

Austin slammed his fist down on the table. "I'm so sick of these assholes."

Mikeis Winston stood up and raised his hand. "Might be a stupid question, but can someone tell me what FDLE means?"

"Florida Department of Law Enforcement," Austin said with a dismissive tone and a flick of his hand. Mikeis sunk back into his seat in the corner of the room. An embarrassed look stretched across his face. He resumed fiddling with his interlaced fingers.

Austin, Kyle, and George's conversation quickly devolved into a shouting match, their yells filling the wooden walls of the barn. Austin slid his chair back and stood up, the leg of his chair burying itself in a pile of hay. He pointed a finger at George. "You're being too soft on these little assholes, man!" He smacked the back of his hand against the palm of his other. "We have to take action."

Ron Hill stepped forward, holding his hands out before him, trying to signal to the other men to stop talking. His colossal frame loomed over the three argumentative men. "That's enough." His voice boomed out over the others. "Y'all fighting with each other won't do a goddamn thing to get justice for our girls!" His cheeks turned a darker shade of magenta with each syllable. His fist slammed down on the table, shaking the legs. The flimsy card table looked like it might give out under the weight of his punch. "These mother fuckers took my little girl from me. There will be fucking justice." His voice cracked under the sustained pressure of his shouts. He took his fist off of the table and slid it into the pocket of his blue jumpsuit. The red faded from his cheeks, and they returned to their normal pale complexion. "We just have to work together to find that justice," he said in a much more subdued tone.

Zach Connolly was sitting in the far corner of the room. His red hair was a tangled mop on his head, and he had been rubbing his chin without saying a word since he sat down twenty minutes ago. The patch of hairless skin between his bottom lip and chin burned red and was beginning to swell from the irritation. Ron wondered if he always rubbed his chin like that or if this was a new tick brought on by stress. Ron considered his own new habit, biting his nails. He had always hated nail biters, but now, he found it oddly soothing. Zach opened his mouth to speak before closing it again.

"You got something you want to say, Zach?" Ron asked.

"Yeah, uh, what if we scared the shit out of them?"

The men looked around at each other. Zach stood up from his chair and strutted across the room; his steel-toed work boots banged off the floor. He stopped a few feet from the table. "We scare the fuck out of them and tell them not to mess with our girls again. We make them apologize to each of us." He shrugged when he finished his sentence.

George leaned forward. "And just how would we do that?"

"Everyone knows that Jackson kid takes all his buddies up to his parents' cabin before the school year starts. Right?" Everyone except Mikeis nodded; he sat there listening with a puzzled look on his face. Being the only single father, and working long hours, he missed out on a lot of the social aspects of the town. He was completely unaware of the trip the football players took, or who they played. In fact, the only reason he was even aware of this conspiracy was because of a friendship he had developed with Austin while they both worked together. Despite Austin leaving the company to start his lawn care business, the two stayed in contact, getting a beer together several times a month. "What if we get together, slash their tires, and spook them real good? When they're scared, we demand they stay away from our girls and apologize to us."

George nodded his head in agreement. "That could work."

Austin broke into a chuckle. It wasn't a normal laugh, like one would expect to hear after telling a joke. This laugh was edged with incredulousness. All the men snapped their heads to look at him. He glared at Zach, a flicker of hatred dancing in his eyes. "You think I want a fucking apology? One of those monsters raped my daughter, you stupid fuck. An apology doesn't mean shit to me. I said I wanted justice." He sprang to his feet and stared into George's eyes. "This isn't kindergarten. An apology means nothing to me now. They need to pay for what they've done to our girls." His teeth gnashed in an animalistic fury.

"I get that, man, but what do you want us to do?" Mikeis asked. "The police won't help us, the FDLE won't help us, the school won't help us, the mayor won't help us. Face it, man, there's nothing we can do."

"We can kill them."

The voice came from behind Ron, causing him to jump. He jerked around to see Jack leaning against the wall. The man had been so quiet that the others forgot he was there. He had his legs and arms crossed, gazing at a spot on the floor with his black Tampa Bay Buccaneers hat pulled low, obscuring his face.

"What did you just say?" Mikeis asked.

Jack repeated himself. "We can kill them." His voice was calm, his tone even. There was no inflection, no hint of sarcasm. Jack looked up from the spot on the barn floor he had been analyzing. "You said it, Mikeis. Ain't nobody helping us."

"Whoa, I didn't say we should kill anyone, man! That's too far," Mikeis said as he held up his hands.

"Is it? You were ready to go along with scaring these boys at that cabin. What do you think would happen once it was all done? You think they'd run back home and change their ways?" Jack pushed himself off the wall and unfolded his arms. He stepped up beside Ron. The lone light dangling in the center of the room illuminated his face. Ron looked at his friend and no longer recognized him.

Jack shook his head. "No. Those boys would go and tell their daddies. Best-case scenario, they make our lives and the lives of our families a living hell. Parking tickets, harassment, bullying, you name it. Worst-case scenario, Chief Sanders gets a wild hair up his ass and arrests us for assaulting a bunch of minors." He shook his head again. "We kill them and destroy the evidence."

He glanced up at Ron. "They took away your little girl, Ron. What do you have to lose?"

Ron's face pulled back in a tight grimace. A tear escaped his eye at the mention of his daughter. He brushed it away and said, "You know I'm with you, Jack."

"You've all gone mad," Zach exclaimed. "We're not fucking murderers; we're not killing anyone!"

Austin clapped his hands together. "Fuck that, I'm in. These bastards are going to pay for what they did to my daughter." He walked around the table and stood next to Ron and Jack.

Jack nodded at Austin. "It's really simple, gentlemen. You have one job on this planet. You are here to protect your children. Every man at this table has failed. Now, me and Ron, our daughters are gone. We don't get to make this right. We don't get a chance to protect them. Each of you," Jack pointed at the remaining men, "you can protect your daughters." He stared at George. "Protect your daughter, George." His glance flicked to Mikeis. "Mikeis, how long until your daughter can't take the bullying?" He looked at Kyle. "Do you think your daughter will ever forgive herself for getting an abortion? We have failed as fathers. The system has failed us. The school has failed us. This town has failed us. It's time we take matters into our own hands."

The room fell completely silent except for the creaking of the building itself. The wood seemed to buckle and scream under the pressure of the decisions they were making. Jack turned around and walked back to the wall he had been leaning against earlier. He retook his position and crossed his arms, awaiting their response.

"How would we do it?" Kyle's whisper seemed to fill the room. A devious smile stretched across Jack's face.

"I have two old vehicles. A '69 Ford and a '73 Pontiac. They're not great, but they run. Neither of them has any computers that can be tracked, like modern cars. From my place to their campground are mostly back roads. I doubt there would be any cameras," Ron said.

Mikeis nodded. "We can't take our phones either. They could ping off a tower or something."

"You're both right," Jack said. "We need to do this low-tech, and we need an alibi. I say we deck this barn out for a poker game. We could all meet here and ride together in Ron's old cars."

"I don't think I want to do this," George said under his breath. "The Bible says thou shall not kill."

"I understand, George. Your daughter was victimized too. If we're going to do this, we all need to be in," Ron said. He leveled his gaze at the man, locking eyes with George. The two men stared at each other for what seemed like an hour before George looked down at the table.

"George, do you want justice for your daughter?"

Austin's voice cut through the tension. George balked at the accusatory tone. He seemed to sink even lower into his seat. "Of course I do."

Austin clapped his hands. "Then it's all settled. How do we do this thing, Jack?"

Jack didn't move from his position on the wall. He buried his thumbs in the pockets of his jeans. "It's just like Ron said. Low tech and an alibi. We cover for each other. I don't think killing them is enough, though."

Mikeis stood up. "What do you mean, killing them ain't enough?"

Jack's wicked smile grew larger.

"We have to make them suffer."

Chapter 19

Justin's shrill cries filled the room. Chase found himself shouting but not comprehending his own words. Droplets of boiling water bounced off Justin's melting face and danced onto Chase's shoulders. He recoiled from the stinging rain and snapped his head down to see the specks on his shoulder turning a fierce shade of red. The masked man finished pouring the pot of boiling water onto Justin and tossed it aside. It clanged against the ground and rolled before coming to a stop at the wall. Chase stole a look at the formerly handsome quarterback. Steam radiated off of him, making it difficult to get a clear view. When the steam cleared, Chase retched at the boy's disfigured appearance. His entire head was as red as their team's jerseys. His skin blistered under the unrelenting heat, and a large boil formed on Justin's cheek. It pulsated momentarily and then exploded from the pressure, coating the left side of Chase's face in a sickly yellowish liquid. Justin's eyelids drooped, barely hanging on by half-melted threads of skin.

Justin gasped for air through his tattered lips. It was a ragged and labored half-breath that reminded Chase of the death rattle his grandfather had wheezed last year. His head slumped forward, and Chase couldn't be sure if the boy was still alive. He tried to fix his eyes on Justin's chest, and after a moment, he saw it. Justin's chest rose a few centimeters. He was still alive.

A part of Chase held out hope someone would rescue them, but another part wished Justin would go into shock and die. Even if someone did save them, Justin's life would never be the same. Years of surgery could never fix his face. He hated the other boys for filming him and posting the video online, but they didn't deserve to die for it, not like this. He wanted Justin to die, not out of hatred or anger, but so he wouldn't suffer any more pain. Chase considered praying for the quarterback's death, but stopped; surely God would frown on such a morbid request. Instead, he prayed for deliverance. He confessed everything he had done wrong in his life, down to the most minor things he could think of.

The slam of the front door interrupted Chase's deep contemplation. He jerked his head in that direction, hoping to see Chief Sanders coming to rescue them. Instead, one man had flung his mask off his face and dashed outside.

"Would you go get him?" Jack commanded in an exasperated tone, waving his large hunting knife toward the door. One of the other masked men shook his head but walked to the door. When this man threw open the front door, Chase could see the man who had left. He was hunched over just off the porch, hands squeezing his knees as he retched into the dirt. The second man pulled the door shut behind him.

Their muffled voices wormed their way through the walls.

"You have to pull yourself together; we're almost done."

"I don't think I can do this," the first man said between gags. "This is too much."

"I get it, man, but we are so close. Why don't you pull it together, and we can go in and end this bullshit?"

A look of discontent spread across Jack's unmasked face. He slapped the flat side of the blade of his hunting knife against his left palm and began pacing.

"Hurry the fuck up," he shouted.

Chase could hear the two men walking across the wooden porch. The door flung open, and the two men re-emerged into the room. They marched across the room and stood on either side of Jack. Jack took the blade in his left hand and held the knife, handle first, to the man who had been throwing up.

"George, why don't you finish off Lemichael?"

George wiped the vomit from his lips and slowly stretched out his hand. His puke-coated fingers wrapped around the handle.

"Come on, George, you were fired up a minute ago," Jack said.

The man who had introduced himself as Ron slid his mask off and tossed it aside. Chase watched as the rabbit head fell gently to the floor. It landed perfectly upright, eyes fixed on the horrid scene.

"Do it, George; you know what they did," Ron commanded.

George approached the boys. Lemichael's head remained slumped forward. He had phased in and out of consciousness ever since they had taken the hot knife to the stubs of his fingers. George gripped Lemichael's shoulder with his left hand, while the knuckles of his right hand turned white against the pressure of squeezing the knife handle.

Tears streamed down his face. A cacophonous roar erupted from the other men as they cheered him on, their words lost in a tribal clamor. Chase watched the man steel himself against the barbarism of the other men; he wanted to scream for George to stop, but the words wouldn't work their way out of his mouth. He watched in horror as George Davis released a sound that landed somewhere between a wail and a squeal before plunging the hunting knife into Lemichael's chest.

George leaned into the blow, throwing his whole body into it, causing the entire blade to submerge into the boy's chest. Lemichael's head snapped up. His eyes widened as the realization of what happened sank in. The boy shrieked, then immediately gasped for air. A gurgled choking noise quickly replaced the gasp. Chase watched as Lemichael convulsed frantically, rocking the chair around in his effort to escape. The desperation in Lemichael's eyes tore a hole in Chase's soul.

George cried out again as he yanked the blade out. He held the blood-drenched knife in front of his face; his eyes burned with rage. George let loose another barbaric howl and launched the knife into Lemichael's chest again. He howled and yelled as he ripped the knife out and plunged it back in again and again. He repeated this slaughter until long after the life drained from Lemichael's eyes and his breathing stopped. George stabbed the body until his own arm failed him. Finally exhaustion settled in, and George slumped to the floor in front of Lemichael. Sobs quickly replaced his furious yells. He sank farther to the ground and gripped Lemichael's blood-soaked shorts.

"I'm sorry," he moaned between sobs. He repeated himself several more times as the other men watched. After a few minutes, Jack reached down and grabbed the knife still embedded in Lemichael's chest and yanked it out. A gush of blood spouted out and coated Jack's arm.

Jack wiped the bloody knife blade against his jumper, revealing the shiny steel of the blade.

"Someone grab him," Jack said as he leaned against the wall. "Pull him together."

Two of the masked men stepped forward and grabbed George by the shoulders, hoisting him to his feet. The men supported all of George's weight since his legs buckled under the exhaustion and emotional fatigue. The trio clumsily made their way across the room and out the door.

Chase could make out George's muffled sobs through the now-closed door. Despite his best efforts, he could not tear his eyes away from Lemichael's lifeless body.

"Jesus Christ, I don't even know what to say. That was fucking intense," Jack said. A grin stretched across his face. He chuckled as he looked around the room. "Has everyone participated in a kill?" Jack spun his head to get a view of the other men. All of them were nodding except for the one man standing in the corner. "Zach?" Jack held out the knife, handle first, toward the silent man. The man shook his head.

"I'll be ready, but until then, nobody touches Chase."

Chase's heart exploded into a furious rhythm. He squirmed in his seat and tried to force his hands free. Jack turned back toward him. He flipped the knife in his hand and pressed the blade against Chase's cheek. It bit into his flesh, but Chase wasn't sure if the blood running down his chin was from the fresh cut or the last of Lemichael's blood on the blade. "Stop squirming." Chase froze in his constraints and locked eyes with Jack. The coldness in his eyes sent a shiver of fear through Chase's entire body.

"Alright, Zach. Chase is all yours." Jack looked back at the masked man in the corner. "But you better do it," Jack said, before turning his attention back toward Chase, "or I'll do it my way." Jack winked at Chase, then returned his gaze to Zach.

Zach nodded. "I'll handle it."

Ron clapped his hands. "Well, alright then, we're almost done here, gentlemen."

Chapter 20

Ron leaned against the front wall of his worn-down barn. He examined the paint peeling in the corners, revealing the rotting wood beneath. Cracks that formed long ago in the deteriorating planks showed the roof supports buckling over his head. The barn had been in his family for three generations. His dad quit caring for the property once his alcoholism set in, and the barn was dead last on the priority list when Ron inherited it. At that moment, he decided that if he escaped this night with his life and freedom, he would fix up this old building. He returned his half-smoked Newport to his lips, then crossed his arms over his red and black checkered shirt. A black truck and a red car made their way over the hill in the distance and drove down the road leading to his farm. He watched them approach, taking deep lungfuls of smoke with each drag of the cigarette. He battled the sense of dread setting in.

The two vehicles passed through his gated entryway and proceeded down the long driveway before stopping in front of the barn. Jack Rivers stepped out of the black F-150. Ron recognized it as an early two thousand model, similar to one he used to own. Austin Thomas slid out of a red Toyota Corolla and retrieved a duffel bag from the back seat. The two men strutted across the lawn without speaking. Ron took one last deep inhale from his cigarette, then tossed it into the dirt at his feet; the burning cherry hissed in the damp soil. Ron stamped the cigarette out with the toe of his boot before pushing himself off the wall. He stuck out his hand toward Jack.

Jack shook Ron's outstretched hand. "You ready to do this?" Jack asked.

Ron grunted and stuck out his hand toward Austin. Austin shook it. "You think the others will show up?"

Ron noticed the slight tremor in Austin's hand but elected not to acknowledge it. He shook his head. "I'm not sure, but I'm going through with this no matter what." Austin nodded in approval and smacked Ron on the shoulder.

"Me too, brother," Austin said.

As if on cue, a dark-colored sedan crested the hill. The roar of the motor rolled through the open terrain.

"Well, I guess that answers my question," Austin said with a chuckle.

Ron pursed his lips together. "I suppose it does. Come on, let's get started." Ron threw the front door of the barn open, and the two men followed him inside. The dying light of the late afternoon sun illuminated the dark barn. Ron stepped off to the side and turned on a light in the corner. It was a square industrial light that rested atop a tripod and cast a powerful beam throughout the room. He walked over to the light switch on the wall and turned on the one light that dangled in the center of the barn. Beneath it sat the table the men had been sitting at just a few days prior, but now it had a green tablecloth draped over it. An ashtray rested in the middle of the table with seven cigars, a lighter, and a cutter beside it. On the floor, between two chairs, was a silver briefcase.

Ron motioned toward the table. "So I planned it all out. We'll smoke the cigars before we leave. In the silver case is a poker set; we can spread the cards out on the table and stack the chips unevenly to make it look like we had been playing all night." He turned toward Jack. "Did you bring the booze?"

"Yeah, it's in the truck. A handle of vodka, two twenty-four packs of Bud Light, a cooler, and ice."

Austin laughed. "You couldn't have gotten a better beer?"

Jack shook his head. "Ain't like we're actually drinking it, smartass."

"Can you two bring it in here?" Ron said, cutting off the bickering. "We can dump out most of the beer, crush the cans, and toss them in the trash can in the corner. Let's leave some half full and leave them around the room so it looks like we got too drunk to finish our beers."

"Oh, and I brought shot glasses for the vodka. Figured we could take a shot to calm our nerves and leave our DNA on the glasses," Jack said.

Ron clapped Jack on the shoulder. "You're a genius, man. We should put the beer cans to our lips in case they want to test them for DNA or something."

Austin tossed his duffel bag into one corner before he took a step toward the door. "Well, let's get started."

Austin and Jack exited the barn. Ron heard them remove the cooler from the truck and the sound of ice being poured into it. He turned away from the entrance and made his way to the poker table. He hoisted the silver briefcase flat onto the table, unclasping it carefully so as not to spill the contents inside when he opened it. The case contained rows of colored poker chips separated by foam lining. He stacked chips at uneven intervals before stacking the playing cards in front of one chair and laying out the big and little blind chips. He heard Austin and Jack shuffling back into the barn. They carried a large, white Igloo cooler. They set it down near the poker table, but closer to the wall.

"Mikeis is here," Austin said.

"Anyone else?"

"I saw two trucks coming over the hill," Jack replied.

"Just missing one more then," Ron said.

"I bet it's the Bible thumper, George," Austin snapped.

"Nah, I have a good feeling about him. I'm worried about Zach Connelly."

Jack looked at Ron. "Why're you worried about him?"

"I'm not sure he'll go through with it, even if he does show up," Ron replied. "The guy just didn't seem committed, ya know?"

"Guess we'll find out soon," Austin said with a shrug.

The three men took turns pouring beer down the drain and pressing the empty beer cans to their lips. Mikeis entered the room without saying a word. He hovered near the doorway and watched them for a minute. Without speaking, he joined them in cracking the beer cans, pouring them down the drain, and pressing the cans to his lips before tossing them in the trash. Shortly after, Kyle Simpson and George Davis entered the room. Kyle immediately mimicked the actions of the other men, while George rubbed at the golden cross on his necklace. He looked at it for a long time before sighing and tucking it into his shirt. He joined the others in their efforts to make the barn look like a guys' night.

Austin gave Ron a backhanded slap on the arm. "Guess you were right about George," he whispered. Ron winked at George and went back to his work.

Just as they had gone through about three-quarters of the beer, the squeak of brakes broke the silence. The men stopped mid-action and watched the door as Zach Connelly entered the room. Just like the others, Zach hesitated by the door. Instead of joining his co-conspirators by the beer cooler, he walked across the room and sat at the poker table. Nearly in unison, the other men finished their robotic motions and tossed their empty beer cans in the trash can. They turned toward Ron and Jack and waited for one of them to speak.

Jack finally broke the silence. "Alright, we're almost done. We're going to smoke these cigars to various lengths, and then we need to take a shot of vodka."

Zach pointed to the bottle. "Why take a shot of vodka?"

Jack smiled. "To make sure our DNA is on the shot glasses, and," he walked up to Zach, "to steel our nerves." The two men locked eyes for a moment, and Jack could see the hesitation in the other man's eyes. Jack turned away and pulled out the shot glasses and the bottle of vodka he had stashed in a bag next to the cooler. He poured seven shot glasses as Ron passed out the cigars, and the men took turns lighting them. Ron took the time to show Austin how to cut and light a cigar since it was the first time he had smoked one. Being the connoisseur he was, Ron taught him a trick to cutting the end just right to avoid getting bits of tobacco in your mouth. Jack watched the scene play out and admired how, under any other circumstances, this would be a fantastic guy's night. Jack shook the thought away and passed out the shot glasses. The men looked down at the clear liquid. Jack held his glass up. "To justice."

Ron, Austin, Kyle, and Mikeis immediately clanked their shot glasses together. George followed after a short pause. Zach didn't move to clink glasses or take his shot. He stared at the little glass in his hand before realizing the other men were waiting for his response. He slowly raised his glass to meet the others. Everyone joined in chanting "to justice." Everyone except Zach.

The men took a few minutes to smoke their cigars before setting them down in the ashtray.

"Ok, I brought the jumpsuits. They're in my car," George said.

Jack eyed Zach suspiciously, wary of the man's apparent apprehension.

"And I brought the machetes," Ron said.

Zach winced at the words, then looked around, hoping nobody noticed. He locked eyes with Jack. Jack's stare sent a shiver running down his spine. Zach leaned forward and poured himself another shot of vodka. He held the glass out in Jack's direction. "One more for the nerves," he said. Zach tilted his head back, allowing the burning liquid to slide down his throat. He slammed the shot glass top down on the table and winked at Jack, desperate to portray a confidence he did not feel. "Good to go," Zach said.

Jack left the group and walked to a large storage closet on the far end of the barn. He pulled open the door, revealing two large metal canisters. Carefully pulling them from the shelves, he carried them back to the table and gently set them down.

"The hell are those?" Mikeis asked.

"These," Jack replied as he patted one of the canisters, "are nitrous oxide." Mikeis gave him a curious look. "I'm a dentist," Jack replied, "but I also have an anesthesiologist who works out of my office. I fudged some numbers in the system to make it look like he was two canisters short. When he ordered these two bad boys, I simply took them and set the numbers back in the system. Ron was kind enough to let me stash 'em here for a few days." He nodded to Ron.

"Ok, and what are we going to do with them?" George asked with a puzzled look on his face.

"If we can corner these little fuckers in a small enough room," he shrugged, "this is enough gas to put them on their asses." Jack hoisted one canister onto the table so the other men could get a better look. "You turn this knob and roll it into a room. They'll be unconscious in a couple of minutes. Then we do what we want."

Kyle smiled. "You're a fucking genius, man. We can seriously fuck them up."

Jack nodded. "There is one little caveat, though: we can't leave them in there too long. Enough exposure could kill them."

Austin laughed. "Bro, I think that's the point."

Ignoring his smartass remarks, Jack continued. "We also have to be careful not to inhale it ourselves."

Ron clapped his hands. "Guess we'll hold our breath then. Everyone ready?"

"One more thing, guys," Austin said. He retrieved a bag he had set in the corner of the room. "In case this whole thing goes tits up, I thought we should wear masks." He opened the bag to reveal seven rabbit masks. "I had these from a play my kid was in when she was five. It seemed like some sort of comedic justice to wear them now."

"Damn, those are creepy as fuck," Kyle said.

"Then it will scare the piss out of those boys," Jack said with a smile.

Ron held his hands up. "Ok, let's go over the plan one more time."

Chapter 21

"Alright, alright," Jack said while holding the knife up. "I think it's my turn; what do you think, guys?"

The men broke into a series of whoops, cheers, and clapping. *They've lost it; they've gone wholly barbaric,* Chase thought. Looking around the room, blood lust entirely consumed the men. Chase recognized their sporadic movements and flexed muscles. They were engulfed in adrenaline and testosterone, the way he and his teammates were before a big game.

Jack waved his hands like a quarterback silencing an unruly crowd and pointed toward the back wall. "Turn the TV back on," he commanded. One of the men grabbed the TV remote and pressed the power button. The blue LED light of the TV filled the room. The TV was still connected to Justin's laptop. A photo of a handsome Justin holding up last year's State Championship trophy adorned the screen. Jack moved the mouse around to wake up the laptop before pulling up a video. He moved the mouse to about the halfway mark and pressed play.

It was the video the boys had watched earlier. The one from the party at Hector's house. The party that led to Kortney Rivers taking her life.

Chase squeezed his eyes shut, desperately trying to avoid the images on the screen. It was bad enough they had forced him to endure the images the first time, but he couldn't stomach the scene again. Unfortunately, he couldn't cover his ears with his hands bound to the chair.

One of the men walked over to him. Chase could sense the man looming over him. He felt a flick to his forehead.

"Open your eyes." The words were spat at him with malice.

Chase immediately obeyed the command. The man in front of him was wearing his mask, but he could tell by the voice and stature that this was the man who had introduced himself as Kyle Simpson. His assailant lingered a moment longer before stepping aside to reveal the screen. The video showed Kortney Rivers's nude body as she lay unconscious on the bed. A hand appeared from off-camera and groped one of her breasts. The camera turned abruptly to reveal the hand belonged to Irish. His red hair was a mess, and he was drenched in sweat. He wore a massive smile and threw up the "rock on" sign with his free hand.

"I think she's smiling. Yeah, she likes it," Irish said into the camera.

Jack Rivers paused the video, freezing Irish's grinning face on the screen. He turned back toward the restrained boys. He tossed the knife back and forth between his hands, then trudged across the room until he was standing in front of Irish. Chase stole a glance at the redhead. Irish's eyes were wide and rimmed with fear. He was shaking so violently that the legs of the chair were tap dancing on the wood flooring.

"N-n-o, don't. I didn't, it was," Irish stammered.

Jack pressed a finger to his lips. "Shhhhh."

Jack raised the knife so it was at eye level with Irish. Irish's mouth stretched into a silent scream. The boy craned his neck in an attempt to avoid the approaching blade. Jack reached around with his other hand and snatched Irish by the hair, jerking his head back. The front legs of the chair momentarily rose under the force before crashing back down.

"I don't see you smiling."

Jack's voice was icy, emotionless.

Chase watched as the realization of what was about to happen flashed in Irish's eyes. Jack stuck the blade of the knife into the boy's mouth. A sickening cracking noise filled the cabin as several of Irish's teeth were shattered and ejected from his mouth. Chase watched the shattered remnants fall to the floor. A flood of tears rolled down Irish's face. In one jerking motion, Jack yanked the blade through Irish's cheek. The gash opened wide and stretched from his ear through the entire length of his mouth. Irish released a gasp, followed immediately by a high-pitched shriek.

"Stop it! You don't have to do this." Chase found his voice again.

"Shut the fuck up," Kyle commanded.

"Please, I'm begging you. Just end it right here! This isn't what your daughters would want!"

Kyle Simpson stepped forward and backhanded Chase across the face.

"Shut the fuck up, kid."

Jack looked over at Chase, a smile stretched across his face. With another violent jerk, he ripped the blade through Irish's other cheek. A splash of blood spurted from the wound and splattered across Justin's chest. Justin raised his head slightly and released a quiet moan before dropping his head again. Chase could clearly see through the gaping wound in Irish's face. Irish thrashed about in the chair, screaming over and over again. Jack patted Irish on the head.

"He's smiling; I think he likes it," Jack Rivers said as he tossed the knife onto the floor. He moved his mouth around for a brief moment before spitting on Irish. A few of the men chuckled.

One of the men crossed the room and picked up the knife. He slid his mask up with the other hand and allowed it to rest on his head. His face was marred by years of hard labor but wore a stern look of resolve. He turned away from the boys and faced the group of men.

"My daughter, Imani, she gets bullied real bad. All the boys on the football team do it. They tell her she's fat. They pretend the earth is shaking when she walks by." His voice quivered. "She started making herself throw up so she could lose some weight." He turned to face Irish. "Put herself in the hospital." His voice was flushed with anger. "She almost died because of you." Spit flew from his lips. He pointed the blade at Irish. "I never want to hear this pig speak again. What do y'all say?"

"Do it, Mikeis," one of the masked men in the back encouraged.

"Stick the fucking pig," shouted another.

Jack Rivers rested a hand on Mikeis's shoulder." It's your call, buddy," Jack assured him.

Mikeis turned around. Stepping forward, he stood over the still-thrashing Irish. He watched as blood ran down Irish's shirt. The boy desperately tried to speak but couldn't work his mouth correctly. In one swift move, Mikeis plunged his left hand into Irish's overly agape mouth and seized the boy's tongue, made easy due to the hydration of the boys' drinking all night. Irish thrashed his head side to side, attempting to dislodge his assailant's grip, but Chase could see the muscles in Mikeis's arm tense as he tightened his grip. Mikeis stuck the knife into Irish's mouth and began sawing back and forth. Justin's bobbing head partially obscured the view of the carnage taking place in Irish's mouth, but Chase could tell Mikeis was taking it slowly. Judging by how easily the blade cut through Irish's cheeks, it was sharp enough to cut through the tongue in one movement, but Mikeis savored it. Irish thrashed up and down, rocking his chair violently from side to side. After a moment, Mikeis stood back up and punched his hand into the air. Some of the men clapped as he triumphantly held up Irish's severed tongue. He tossed it to the floor at the boy's feet, where it landed with a meaty flop.

Mikeis held the knife out at his side and waited for someone to take it. Ron Hill stepped forward. He gripped the handle and slid it from Mikeis's hand. Mikeis lingered for a moment longer, taking in the wreckage of Irish's mangled mouth, before reluctantly stepping aside. Now Ron's impressive frame stood in front of Irish.

"I already talked about it earlier, but my daughter, Taylor, she committed suicide." Ron choked down a sob. "She did it after you," he paused and looked at Jack, "after you did what you did to Kourtney." He wiped a tear from the corner of his eye, leaving a trail of blood smudged across his face. "So, it only seems fair that you suffer a similar fate."

Ron bent over and stuck the blade into Irish's right arm, just below the elbow. A rush of crimson blood bubbled to the surface, spilling over the side of his arm and draining onto the floor. Ron dragged the blade down the length of the forearm, stopping at the base of the hand. Irish responded with a series of hysterical sobs and incoherent protests. Methodically, Ron removed the blade from the forearm and plunged it into the other. Again, he dragged the blade down the length of the arm and stopped at the hand. He pulled the blade out and handed it back to Jack. Jack made a swiping motion with the blade, which sent a stream of blood onto the floor. Ron gripped both of Irish's forearms.

The blood seeped through his fingers and coated his hands. He leaned in so close to Irish's face that their noses brushed against each other's.

"Now, you spend the last few minutes of your miserable life thinking about what you did and all of the pain it has caused." He released Irish's forearms and stood up. He raised his foot and pressed it against Irish's chest. Ron shifted his weight forward. The chair rocked back on its back legs. "I hope you burn in hell." Ron pushed.

Irish crashed backward onto the floor. Chase snapped his head to the left, catching glimpses of Irish between Justin's head bobbing as he gasped for air. Irish's mouth hung ajar. The nub of his tongue danced frantically in his blood-soaked mouth. Blood poured from his open forearms and pooled all around him. Chase watched as Irish stopped fighting the inevitable. A look of acceptance washed over him, and within minutes, he stopped breathing.

Chapter 22

Chase fought to catch his breath. His chest rose and fell at an increasingly rapid pace. He fixated on Irish's lifeless body sprawled on the floor to his left, rivers of blood still trickling down his arms. The thrashing Irish had done when first kicked over caused the blood to coat his face and dye his pale skin a pinkish color. That blood was now congealing into a grotesque Jello-O.

Beside him, Justin groaned through partially melted lips. Bits of his lips clung together, creating a morbid kind of string. His blistered skin oozed sickly secretions, causing him to reflect the bits of morning sunlight cracking through the window.

Chase couldn't believe the boy was still alive. "Hang in there, man," he said.

"Why should he?" one of the men in the back asked. Chase couldn't tell which of the men had said it. "He's fucked anyway," another stated.

"There's always hope," Chase said with every bit of defiance he could muster, which admittedly wasn't much at this point.

A couple of the men laughed at the sentiment.

"Boy, haven't you figured out that you're going to die here?" Chase turned his head to look Jack Rivers in the eye. Chase thought of the old saying "The eyes are the windows to the soul" but couldn't remember where he had heard it or who said it. If it was true, Jack Rivers didn't have a soul. Not anymore, at least.

Holding the monster's gaze, he said, "Maybe, but you'll get caught and spend the rest of your life in prison. You assholes killed the chief's sons. What do you think they're going to do to you? You'll be lucky if you make it to prison."

Jack cracked another smile. He rested a hand on Chase's head and ruffled his hair like a child.

"I'm already in a prison. I have been since my daughter killed herself." He allowed his hand to fall off of Chase's head. "It's almost time, guys. The sun's coming up; we gotta get this show moving." Jack paced back and forth in front of the remaining two boys. "This all started because of you." He stopped pacing in front of Justin and pointed at him. "All of this pain is because of you." Jack leaned forward and rested his hands on his knees. "Your dead friends? That's your fault. My dead daughter? Your fault." He poked Justin in the forehead each time he said the word "fault." His finger dipped unnaturally deep into Justin's melted flesh each time he poked him. "But there is some good news, kid; you have an opportunity to apologize. You can apologize to me, to these other dads, and I'd probably apologize to Chase for getting him killed right along with you."

Chase sucked in a deep breath when Jack said the last part. Jack cocked his head toward Chase and winked.

"Alright, Justin. I know you're dying and all that, but here's your chance to repent. Consider this your confessional. I mean, after all, I *AM* a father." He paused. "Or at least was. I'll make you a deal. If you apologize to us, I'll end it quick. If you don't want to apologize, well, let's just say that would suck for you."

Jack reached toward Justin's mouth and gripped the corners, forcing his lips to pucker out. The skin around his jaw peeled away, revealing the muscles underneath. Justin cried out in agony. He pushed Justin's head up before yanking his hand away. Melted bits of flesh ripped away and clung to Jack's fingers. Jack wiped the melted skin on his blue jumpsuit and said, "Jesus Christ, that's fucking disgusting." Justin looked like he was crying, but no tears fell down his disfigured face.

"Seriously, that was fucking gross, man. I guess you won't be much of a hit with the ladies anymore." Jack shrugged his shoulders. "Sorry about that."

Jack stood upright and took a step back. "Time to apologize."

Justin sucked in a deep breath through his tattered mouth. "I...I'm," he gasped. Jack's twisted smile returned to his face. "I'm not fucking sorry," Justin blurted out.

Chase's jaw hit his chest. Jack stepped back as if a wave had hit him, and his smile vanished.

"Your whore of a daughter loved what we did to her. She moaned with pleasure! The rest of you have raised sluts and bitches!"

Justin gasped for air after shouting. The blisters on his skin burst open under the tension of his muscles. Chase turned his attention to their attackers, expecting them to lurch forward. He expected them to rip Justin to pieces with their bare hands, but none of the men moved. Chase watched in disbelief as Justin sucked in another gulp of air and continued.

"Fuck you and your daughters!" Justin pressed his lips together and spit as far as he could, launching the ball of saliva far enough to land at Jack's feet.

Jack looked down at the spit at his feet. He nodded his head and rubbed at his chin. When he looked back up at Justin, that wicked smile returned. "This is going to suck for you." Without breaking eye contact, he held his hand out. One of the men slid the handle of the knife into his palm, and Jack's fingers wrapped tightly around the hilt. He looked at the blood-stained hunting knife as he spoke. "I was going to finish it quick. One fast slash across the throat, ya know?" He stepped forward and grabbed the waistband of Justin's shorts. Justin attempted to squirm away, but Jack yanked the shorts down to expose Justin's flaccid penis.

Justin's eyes shot up to meet Jack's.

"No, no, no, please," Justin pleaded.

"I warned you," Jack chided.

Chase clenched his eyes shut as Jack's free hand wrapped around Justin's penis. With eyes locked, Jack slid the blade down before yanking it up violently. Justin released a small sigh, followed by an agonized wail. When Chase opened his eyes, he saw Jack toss the severed member back at Justin. Justin's screams reverberated off the walls of the cabin. Justin thrashed in his seat, causing the legs of the chair to dance as he attempted to break free. His severed penis smacked the wood floor with a splat. Blood soaked his basketball shorts and ran down his legs. The boy squealed in horror at his emasculation. Eventually, his breathing reduced to dramatic wheezing. The chaotic smack of the chair legs against the floor died down, and Justin's head slumped forward.

Chase quietly thanked God the boy had lost consciousness. He examined the puddle of blood at Justin's feet, then glanced back toward Irish's now-stiff body. The puddles of blood were nearly the same size. Chase couldn't remember how much blood was in the human body, but he knew Justin had to be pretty close to bleeding out. Even though he felt guilty about it, Chase was grateful the young man's suffering was finally coming to an end.

Jack turned to face the other men and raised his arms out to either side like a hellish messiah. The knife dangled loosely from his right hand. "Everyone, take your pound of flesh."

Without hesitation, Austin threw off his mask and snatched the knife from Jack's hand. He rushed over to the unconscious Justin and dragged the blade across his right pectoral muscle. The knife dug deep, allowing the skin to peel back and expose the red sinew of severed muscle fibers. Streaks of blood ran down Justin's stomach and melded into the pool of blood around his crotch.

Austin released a gleeful giggle. He turned around and held out the knife. Ron stepped forward and grabbed it. He dragged the blade across Justin's shoulder. After a moment of admiring his handy work, he passed the blade to the next person. Chase had no choice but to watch as the men took turns digging the knife into various parts of Justin's limp body. Each man, except the one in the corner, took his pound of flesh. By the time they were done, they had reduced the formally handsome, athletic quarterback to a bloody mess of a body. Justin's wheezes grew shallower and more spread out. The color faded from the burned flesh on his face.

When they were done, Jack motioned for the rabbits to come closer to Justin. The murderers, except the man standing alone in the corner, the one Chase knew was Zach Connolly, surrounded Justin. Chase could no longer see the boy, just the back of bloody jumpsuits as they crowded around. A wet cough filled the room. When the men moved away from Justin, Chase could see Justin's head rocked backward; a deep laceration stretched across his neck. A bit of blood spurted from a severed artery and stained the recliner. The next burst of blood was much less powerful, landing primarily on Justin's chest. A slight bubbling at the the wound followed that gush. Then nothing.

Chase knew the boy was dead, and he was up next.

Chapter 23

After a long pause, Jack turned toward the man standing in the corner of the room. The man slid his mask off, and just as Chase suspected, it was Zach Connolly. Megan's dad looked very different from the strict but polite man Chase used to know. The man's pale skin carried a sickly green tint to it, and large bags had formed under his eyes. Chase couldn't be sure, but it looked like the man had lost a significant amount of weight. Zach walked across the room until he was in front of Chase and squatted down so the two were at eye level.

"I'm not going to beg," Chase said as he allowed a final tear to roll down his face. He refused to blink, electing to look his soon-to-be murderer in the eyes.

"I know." Zach's voice was full of resignation, and Chase got the sense the man didn't want to go through with this. A small flame of hope reignited in Chase's chest. Zach leaned in and hugged the boy. It was an odd gesture, given the circumstances, made even stranger by the fact that one was here to kill the other. Zach whispered in his ear, "Megan had a complication." The small flame of hope was extinguished in a flood of panic.

Zach pulled away from the boy and held him at arm's length. Chase balked at the words. "What kind of complication?"

Zach hung his head and said, "I don't know, kid. I'm not a doctor. Something to do with her blood pressure." When he looked back up, tears were pouring down his face. The older man sucked in a raspy breath before continuing. "She didn't make it."

Chase stared in shocked silence. He now understood why Zach was here. The grief piercing his heart was enough to make him murderous as well. That final tear turned into a river. Zach reached down and wiped the tears away.

"I loved her," Chase finally squeaked out. "I never meant for any of this to happen. I need you to believe me. I didn't know about the tape."

Zach patted him on the thigh. "I know, buddy."

"Then why are you doing this?" Chase's voice was pleading now.

Zach shook his head. "I wanted to make sure it went easy for you."

The color in Chase's face drained. "You know, I won't say anything about this. You can let me go, and I swear I'll tell them I don't know who did it. I'll tell them it was men in masks. They don't need to know!"

Zach shook his head again. "It's not that simple, son." He looked back at the other men, then turned back toward Chase. "These men aren't about to risk it."

Chase's shoulders slumped. Defeated, he asked, "Can I have a minute to prepare?"

"Sure, buddy, whatever you need."

Chase lowered his head. "Our father, who art in heaven, hallowed be thy name. Thy Kingdom come, thy will be done, on Earth as it is in Heaven. Give us this day our daily bread, and forgive us our trespasses, as we forgive those who trespass against us. Lead us not into temptation, but deliver us from evil." He paused and glanced up at the men around him. He bowed his head again. "For thou art the power and the glory forever, Amen." Chase hadn't thought himself very religious before today's events. His dad had dragged him to Catholic church for mass his entire life. He always hated those services; he would be bored out of his mind and desperately trying to stay awake. He longed to attend another service with his dad.

Chase looked back up at Zach. "Mr. Connolly, one more thing?"

"Yeah?" Zach eyed him curiously.

"The lock screen on my phone has a picture of Megan. It's on the table over there. Would it be ok if you set it on my lap while it happens?"

Zach stood up and walked to the end table at the far end of the room. He grabbed the cell phone and pressed the power button on the side. The screen illuminated, displaying a picture of his smiling daughter. Zach smiled at her beautiful face, then laid the phone in Chase's lap and pressed the power button again when the screen darkened.

"You ready?"

Chase nodded. "Just do it."

Zach moved around behind Chase. He rested his hand on Chase's head, rubbing the boy's hair. Zach put the knife to Chase's throat. The blade lightly bit into the soft skin, drawing a few droplets of blood. Chase could hear Zach cry behind him. The knife bit in a little deeper, and Chase sucked in a breath. Without warning, Zach pulled the blade away from Chase's neck. "Could y'all give us some privacy? The boy doesn't deserve to die in front of an audience."

Jack eyed him suspiciously. He took a step toward Chase before Ron grabbed him on the shoulder. "Give him the privacy, man. What's he going to do?"

Jack shrugged Ron's hand away. "Oh, I don't know, maybe stab us in the fucking back? I knew you were full of shit. You never had the balls to go through with it."

"Fuck you," Zach snarled. "I'm going to do what has to be done. But we already learned the kid didn't hurt any of your daughters. This is between me and the kid."

Austin reached forward and grabbed Jack's other arm. "Relax. We'll wait outside. Just hurry it the fuck up, we're almost out of time." Austin pointed to the window, where rays of sunshine were fighting their way through the curtains. Jack relaxed his posture and allowed Ron and Austin to pull him toward the door.

"Come on, guys," he said. "Let's give the two their privacy." Jack held the front door as the others filed out. Jack looked back at Zach as the last man exited the room. "You've got two minutes."

"Understood," Zach replied sharply.

"Oh, and Zach? Don't make me regret this." Jack's sinister tone had returned.

Zach nodded. "Wouldn't dream of it."

Jack pulled the door shut with a bang.

Zach waited a moment then released a deep sigh. He squatted down behind Chase and whispered in his ear.

"We don't have much time, so don't speak. This is wrong. I was so distraught about Megan's death that I thought I needed to inflict that pain on you. I was wrong, Chase. You don't deserve this." Zach wedged the blade between the arm of the chair and Chase's forearm. He moved the blade back and forth, severing the silver duct tape. When Zach peeled the tape away, it took all of Chase's arm hair with it. The stinging sensation caused his eyes to water, but he gladly accepted it over the alternative. He stared at his freed arm incredulously as the blood rushed back to his hand.

"Are...are you letting me go?" he stammered.

"Yes," Zach replied as he ran the blade along the tape binding Chase's right leg. "Listen, these are a bunch of middle-aged men. You can outrun them." Zach moved around to the other side of the chair and finished freeing Chase.

Chase tried to stand up, but his legs buckled under his weight. His body had grown stiff and weak from being restrained for hours.

Zach caught him under the arms and hoisted him to his feet. "I know it hurts. You have to pull yourself together. We'll only get one shot at this."

Chase steadied himself. "I'm good."

Zach released Chase, taking a moment to look him in the eyes. "I'm so sorry for the way we treated you. Before all of this, I mean." He waved his hand around the room. "I should have treated you more like a son; you're a great kid."

Chase choked back the tears. "I really loved your daughter, Mr. Connolly."

Zach pulled Chase in for a hug. He squeezed the boy as tight as he could. "I know you did." Zach pulled away from Chase and held him at arm's length. "I'm going to go through the door first and distract them. I need you right behind me, ok? I'll give you the signal, and you run as hard as you can. You clear that porch and get to the trees." Zach pointed at the front door. "If you just keep running in that direction, you'll hit the main road. If you don't see any cars, veer to the left and run until you hit the town. Do not stop until you find help. Do you understand me?"

"Yes, sir," Chase said through a sniffle. "Come out on your signal, run for the trees until I hit the road. If there are no cars, go left and don't stop till I hit the town," Chase repeated.

"Then let's go," Zach said firmly.

"Oh, and Mr. Connolly," Chase said, "thank you."

Zach nodded. "On the count of three."

Chapter 24

The front door of the cabin swung open and hit Kyle squarely on the nose. He staggered backward before falling hard on his ass but sat up quickly to reveal his flattened nose expelling a sea of red blood.

"What the—" Ron started to say, but Zach sprinted through the open doorway before he could complete his thought. Zach reached the end of the porch before any of the other men could react. He propelled himself off the first step, launching toward Ron. The two men collided, crumpling into a heap in front of the stairs.

As soon as the two men hit the ground, Zach shouted, "Now!"

On command, Chase emerged from the cabin and sprinted toward the two men. In the confusion, Zach managed to climb on top of Ron, pinning him to the ground. Chase hit the end of the porch and leaped over the wrestling men. He landed hard in the dirt, sending a shockwave rumbling up his legs and into his lower back before his legs gave out. He fell to his knees, the dirt and gravel ripping at the skin. Pain tore through his legs from the wound. Pushing through the pain, he scrambled to his feet only to lose his balance again. His momentum carried him forward, burying his chin in the dirt. A burning sensation radiated across his face. Chase rested there momentarily, trying to gather the strength to get up again.

"Run, Chase!" The desperation in Zach's voice snapped him back to the present.

Chase glanced back to see a bloodied Kyle and furious-looking Austin jump off the porch. Chase pushed hard with his hands, lifting his chest off the ground like he had done during so many football drills. He found his footing and sprinted toward the tree line. The early morning sun was shining through the trees now, allowing Chase to see clearly into the forest. With such clear visibility, he knew he wouldn't be able to hide; this would be a foot race.

He aimed for the largest opening through the brush. It looked like it may have been an old footpath, long ago overgrown with bushes. It just so happened this particular path began between the two trees prominently displaying his dead friends.

Just before crossing the threshold into the trees, he glanced over his shoulder. Zach still had the upper hand on the much bigger Ron. He watched as Zach reared back his fist and slammed it down on Ron's cheek.

Chase dashed between the two large trees holding up Ford's and Nick's lifeless corpses. He leaped over some thick bushes like a hurdler at a track meet and landed gracefully on both feet. The stiffness in his muscles subsided with each step. He leaned forward and ran harder.

The crack of a pistol ripped through the air. Chase stutter-stepped, nearly losing his footing. He risked one last glance over his shoulder. Although partially obscured by trees, shrubbery, and the men pursuing him, he could make out Zach's body slumped lifelessly on the ground. Jack Rivers stood above him, holding a revolver. Gray smoke wafted from the barrel. Chase watched as Jack shook his head then raised the gun and pointed it in Chase's direction.

The air left Chase's lungs as he realized Megan's father had just sacrificed himself so he could have a chance at escape. He turned his attention away from the murder and continued running toward the road. He slipped around a large oak tree; the tree branches ripped at his skin and whipped his face.

Tree bark exploded inches from his face, sending debris crashing into him. He heard the gunshot a fraction of a second later. He ducked but didn't stop running. Snapping sounds filled his ears as bullets whizzed around him, only to be drowned out by the crack of the pistol filling the air. He could tell the shots were close by their noise and the dirt being kicked up around him. A bullet crashed into another tree to his left. He racked his brain, desperately trying to remember how many shots he had heard. Being a Florida native, he was familiar with guns and knew the revolver only held six rounds. When he didn't hear another shot, he assumed Jack was out of ammunition.

Chase leaped over a ditch. Behind him, Kyle lost his footing and crashed into the ditch. Chase heard an "Oof" as Kyle's chest impacted the ground.

"Get up!" George shouted at Kyle as he leaped over the ditch and dropped to a knee. He raised his hunting bow and aimed at Chase's back. Yanking the bowstring back, he raised his aim slightly, trying to account for the distance Chase was gaining on them. He sucked in a deep breath, held it, then released the arrow.

The arrow whizzed over Chase's left shoulder, missing him by mere inches. Instinctively, Chase ducked as the arrow embedded itself in the tree in front of him. He looked back to see Kyle climbing out of the ditch. Beside him, George remained on a knee, drawing another arrow. Panicked, he turned and continued sprinting in the direction Zach had instructed him to go.

A second arrow whizzed by his head. This one brushed against his face before disappearing into the bushes. Chase felt the sting of the arrowhead tear the flesh on his right cheek but wouldn't allow himself to stop running. Warm, fresh blood spilled from the wound and flowed down his neck.

Run.

Run.

Run.

He thought the word to himself like a mantra, willing his legs to keep moving. His bare feet screamed in agony as the debris on the forest floor continued battering them. His chest tightened as he sucked in gasps of air. He wasn't sure how much longer he could continue running; he couldn't believe these older men were keeping up with him. For a moment, he considered taking his chances with fighting them, but a sound propelled him forward.

A car.

He could hear the engine of a car rumbling in the distance. It reminded him of his dad's old, beat-up truck. It was close enough that he could hear the scrape of the brakes as it rounded the corner. The realization he was so close to the road filled him with a renewed sense of vigor. He forced himself to go faster, pumping his legs as hard as he could. His muscles ached from the effort and his lungs felt like they would burst in his chest, but he pushed on.

Behind him, he could hear Kyle shouting but couldn't make out the words. It sounded like his two pursuers were falling farther behind. Chase tore through a thicket of bushes to reveal an embankment with a metal guardrail at the top.

He had made it.

He threw himself onto the steep embankment. The angle of the hill threatened to send him sprawling backward toward his assailants. Flashes of football practice ran through his mind, Coach Chevy's country twang-laden voice ringing in his ears. "It's all about leverage, son! God dang boy, you need to have a low center of gravity so you don't go backward when you get hit." He dropped his hips and buried his hands in the dirt of the hillside. As he continued to bear crawl up the hill, another car zipped by on the road above him. He was so close he could smell the exhaust fumes. He clawed his way up the last few feet, finally reaching the top of the hill, and gripped the top of the guardrail.

A smile threatened at the edges of his mouth. Despite all the horrors he had endured over the last several hours, he had persevered.

He pulled his legs underneath him and prepared to jump over the railing. Just as his feet left the ground, something struck him in the back of the neck, causing his head to snap forward. His face smacked against the top of the guardrail. The impact sent the world into complete darkness.

He collapsed onto the ground in front of the guardrail and slid back down the hill. He tried desperately to grab onto something, anything, to arrest his fall, but his hands and arms weren't responding to his commands. After sliding backward for a few seconds, he stopped at the base of the embankment.

Slowly, his vision returned. His brain screamed for him to stand up, but his body wasn't responding. He found himself staring to his left, unable to move any part of his body. Footsteps crunched the surrounding leaves. Again he tried to raise himself up, but his arms rested uselessly to either side of him.

"Holy fuck, you shot him in the neck," one of his pursuers said through gasps of air.

Chase wasn't sure who had said it, but the words sent a knife of realization through his mind. There was only one part of playing football that scared him, and his worst nightmare had come true. He was paralyzed. An arrow must have struck him in the spine. He gasped for air but found his lungs weren't responding either. Blood seeped from his mouth and pooled around his face.

"Let's get him back to the cabin," Kyle said, still trying to catch his breath.

George placed his foot at the base of Chase's neck and gripped the arrow. He yanked on the arrow, tearing it out of the injured boy. The pull lifted Chase's limp body off the ground slightly before it crashed back down again.

"Damn, the arrowhead broke off," George complained. "Poor kid."

They rolled Chase onto his back. He found himself staring up at his murderers, unable to move, breathe, or run. He tried to speak, but nothing happened. As a last resort, he blinked his eyes.

George leaped away from him. "Fuck! He's still alive!" he yelled.

"No fucking way?" Kyle asked. Kyle leaned forward, then leaped backward when Chase blinked again. "God damn, this kid is tough!"

In his head, Chase begged the men to end this. He felt himself drowning in his own blood. There was no pain, but the thought of suffocating struck more fear into him than this entire ordeal had. This was the worst way he could imagine going out; he just wanted them to end it quickly.

"What do we do?" Kyle asked.

"Do you have the knife? Or a machete?" George asked. Chase could hear a tinge of remorse in the older man's voice. Tears subtly built up in the corners of Chase's eyes.

"Do I look like I have a knife or a machete? The kid jumped off the porch and I hauled ass after him. Stab him with another arrow or something." Kyle motioned to his disfigured nose and the dried blood coating his face.

George sighed. "I can't." He held up the arrow he had pulled from Chase's neck. "This was my last one. Poor fucking kid. Let's just get him back to the cabin." George bowed his head and said a silent prayer, then reached down and grabbed Chase under the arms. He pulled Chase into a sitting position, which caused Chase's head to loll backward. With Kyle's help, George managed to get Chase onto his shoulder. Exhausted, the two men started the long trek back to the cabin.

Chase found himself staring down George's back as the man carried him through the woods. Darkness crept in from the corners of his vision. One last tear clung to the corner of his eye. Unable to wipe it away, it dangled there for a moment longer before falling onto the forest floor below.

His last thought as the darkness took over was of Megan's smiling face and the life they could have had together.

Chapter 25

George emerged from the tree line first, Chase's deceased body slumped over his shoulder. Kyle stepped out of the trees behind him to see Austin and Jack rolling Zach's body onto its stomach. Ron sat against the side of the cabin while Mikeis nursed his battered face. Even from across the field, George could see the swelling in Ron's left eye.

"Thank God you caught the little fucker," Ron said in an angry tone. He shoved Mikeis's hand away and pushed himself off the ground.

"Yeah, George shot him in the fucking neck with his bow and arrow," Kyle excitedly replied. He raised his arms up and pretended to draw an arrow on an imaginary bow. He made a whooshing sound with his mouth as he let his pretend arrow loose. "Dropped him right as he was about to make it to the road. It was fuckin' sick."

George didn't respond. He lumbered forward, exhausted from carrying the lifeless body back to the cabin. Walking past the other men to the stairs, he sucked in a deep breath before hazarding the first step. His legs shook under the pressure. George feared they might buckle under the weight, but Kyle appeared at his side.

"Let me help you," he said. Kyle gripped Chase by the legs. Carefully, George slid the body from his shoulder and gripped it under the arms, locking his arms across the boy's chest. Chase's arms flopped around with each step. The two men carried the body into the cabin and laid it down in the center of the living room.

George caught the wretched scent of shit, piss, and blood. He forced down a gag, then sucked in a breath through his mouth, trying to avoid the putrid odor. Kyle smacked him on the shoulder. "It's done, man."

Jack stepped through the open doorway, followed by Ron, Austin, and Mikeis.

"Nearly done," Jack corrected.

"What the fuck are we going to do now?" Mikeis asked.

"We stick to the plan," Jack answered.

"In case you haven't noticed, the plan is fucked," Austin said, throwing his hands up in a defeated fashion. "Zach screwed it all up."

Mikeis stepped forward. "Jack, we gotta do something. I can't go to prison. I'm all my daughter has."

Jack held up his hands. "I have an idea. Everyone just chill the fuck out."

"What's the plan?" Ron asked. He pinched his nose and tilted his head back, trying to stop the flow of blood. It made his voice sound like a muppet.

Jack dug a set of car keys out of his pocket. He tossed them to Austin. Austin caught them and held them up.

"You guys go back to the barn and get Zach's car, then bring it here," Jack commanded. "He was never at our poker game. He came here, murdered these guys, then offed himself." Jack pointed to Mikeis. "You're going to help me cut these assholes out of their chairs and dump them on the floor. When we're done, we need to get those bodies off the trees and pull them inside." Jack motioned toward the master bedroom. "Ron, you get the laughing gas canisters out of that bedroom and load them into the other car. George, I need you to strip Zach's body. Make sure there's nothing on him that can be traced back to us. When you're done, wipe down the pistol and put it in Zach's hand. Gotta get his fingerprints all over it. Oh, and find a way to file off the serial number. Does everyone understand their assignments?"

The men nodded and proceeded with their tasks. Austin, Kyle, and George disappeared through the front door, while Mikeis handed the knife to Jack. Mikeis grabbed the chair Lemichael's corpse rested in. Jack took a knee in front of the throne of death. He took a deep breath before cutting the tape holding the body to the chair. When finished, Mikeis pushed the chair forward, and Lemichael's body slumped out of the chair, collapsing onto the floor with a thud. The pair continued their gruesome work on the remaining boys, discarding their bodies on the floor like trash.

Ron emerged from the master bedroom, carrying the gas canisters. He paused near the door. "What are we going to say about me and Kyle having busted noses?"

Jack looked up at his friend. Bruising radiated outward from Ron's mangled nose. His left eye was nearly swollen shut. "Kyle accused you of cheating during the poker game. Y'all got into a fight. Me and Mikeis broke it up. Right, Mikeis?"

Mikeis nodded. "That's right. One helluva fight too."

Ron nodded. "I'll fill Austin and Kyle in when they get back," he said as he stepped through the open door.

Once the bodies were distributed around the living room, Jack stepped outside. He breathed in the fresh air, trying to purge the smell of death from his nostrils. The two remaining bodies hung desecrated in the trees in front of him. He leaned back through the doorway to summon Mikeis. "Come on, we have to get those bodies out of the trees. Bring the hammer."

Together, the two men jogged across the open lawn. Jack reached Ford first. The body hung by its hands, internal organs spilled everywhere. Jack eyed the remains while he waited for Mikeis to catch up. Mikeis came up behind him and said, "Wow, I haven't really gotten a good look at him in the daylight. I can't believe we did this."

Jack sighed. "Well, we did. Now give me a boost so I can get him down."

Mikeis interlocked his fingers, allowing Jack to step up onto his hands. Jack proceeded to pull the nail from the center of the dead boy's hands. Ford's body collapsed to the floor with a sickening squelch. The sign on his chest became dislodged and fell away. Mikeis picked up the sign, turning it over in his hands and reading his own writing. He tossed the sign onto Ford's body. The two men repeated the process for Nick's headless corpse. They grabbed onto Nick's arms and dragged him into the cabin. It took much longer to do the same with Ford's humongous body. The signs managed to stay on Ford as they dragged him. When they were done, they left a trail of gore stretching from the trees to the cabin.

"What about the head?" Mikeis asked.

"Yeah, it's behind the tree Nick was in. We should bring that in too," Jack replied.

"I'll go get it," Mikeis whispered. Jack could hear the regret already bubbling up in the man's voice. There were moments, fleeting as they were, where Jack felt that same pang of regret. When those moments came, he pictured his daughter's body in a casket and was able to push the feeling aside. He knew Mikeis didn't have quite the same image to rely on since his daughter was still alive.

Once done cleaning up their grotesque butchery of the seven high school kids, the men sat on the top step of the porch. After a few minutes, two cars drove down the dirt driveway and stopped in front of the cabin. Austin and Kyle emerged from the vehicles in their bloody jumpsuits.

"It's done," Austin said. "We cleaned up any sign that Zach was with us last night."

With the entire group back together, Jack summoned them all back into the cabin. The men stood in a semicircle around the living room, the massacre they created splayed out before them. Nick's headless corpse. Ford's shredded body. Lemichael's finger's discarded about. Irish's red hair soaked in blood. Hector with a massive hole in his head. Justin's melted flesh. And finally, Chase's now-cold body.

"We've all killed someone here." Jack paused to look each of the other men in the eyes. "No matter what happens, we stick to the story. If one of us fucks this up, we'll all spend the rest of our lives in prison."

A loud sob interrupted him. Jack snapped his head in George's direction. George hunched forward with his hands on his knees, fighting against the impending panic attack. The realization of what they had done had finally set in.

"Pull yourself together, man," Jack ordered. "It's too late for that shit now."

George wiped the tears from his face. He stood back up. "I'm good. Sorry, guys."

Jack continued. "Alright. Everyone knows the story. We were at Ron's house playing poker all night. Ron and Kyle got in a fight. Zach was never there. He must have driven over here, killed them," Jack pointed at the bodies on the floor, "then blew his own head off from the guilt. Everyone good?"

The men answered with an assortment of affirmations.

"Good. Now, let's burn this bitch to the ground." Jack led the men out of the house. Popping the trunk of the car, he pulled out two gas cans and carried them back into the house. He proceeded to pour gasoline onto the bodies in the living room, the smell of gasoline intertwining with the stench of death. Jack created a trail of gas leading from the bodies to the front porch, where he emptied the remaining gas into a large puddle by the stairs. Tossing the empty can to Kyle, Jack picked up the other can. He walked around the cabin, coating the outside in gas. Jack did his best to cover as much of the house as he could, even managing to splash some onto the roof.

With the second gas can nearly empty, he wordlessly walked to Zach's car. He dumped the remaining gas into the front seat before returning the now-empty can to the trunk of their car. He stepped up to the front porch. Kyle, Austin, Mikeis, Ron, and George stood in a straight line behind them.

Jack pulled a pack of matches from his pocket and removed a single match. Striking it, Jack stared into the flame. The fire danced before his face, illuminating the hatred in his eyes. He stretched out his arm and dropped it into the puddle of gasoline at his feet.

The gasoline immediately ignited. Fire rushed forward, following the river of gas into the cabin. Flames erupted from within the building and spewed out of the doorway. In a matter of minutes, fire engulfed the entire cabin.

One by one, the men turned away from the flames. They took turns getting into the car, until Jack stood alone before the hellfire he created.

"Jack! Let's go!" Ron shouted.

Jack turned from the cabin and jogged across the lawn to the waiting car. He paused to strike another match, which he tossed into Zach's car. The vehicle erupted. The heat was so intense it singed the hairs on his forearm before he could move away. He climbed into the car, allowing Kyle to drive them away from their vengeance. Jack watched in the rearview mirror as the cabin burned and a plume of smoke bellowed upward into the sky.

They made it back to Ron's barn without further incident. The men climbed out of their respective vehicles and entered the old wooden structure. The poker table and mess of drinks were strewn about, creating the illusion they had been partying all night. None of the men seemed to be fully alert, instead meandering around the room like zombies, the shock of the past several hours overwhelming their senses. While some of the men paired up, Austin went straight for the bottle of vodka sitting on the table.

He uncapped it, took a big swig, then slammed the bottle on the table. Shaking his head, he walked to the wall at the back of the barn. He steadied himself against it with both hands and released a sob, then slapped himself in the face.

"Austin, you good?" Ron asked.

"Yeah. I'm fine. Give me a goddamn second," he snapped.

"No problem," Ron muttered.

Ron walked to the center of the room and clapped his hands to get everyone's attention. "I know we just had a really long night, but the work ain't done yet. We need to finish covering this up. We still have to burn these uniforms, hide the weapons, and take another shot."

Mikeis stepped toward Ron. "Why do we need to do another shot?"

"In case the cops suspect us, we have booze in our systems. It looks like we've been here drinking all night."

Mikeis wasn't sure the answer made any sense but nodded anyway.

Mimicking Ron, Jack clapped his hands.. All of the men turned to face him. "We're at the finish line. We just need to push a little further.

Everyone step outside and strip off your uniform. Me and Kyle will burn them back at my place. Austin and Mikeis, Ron dug a ditch about a hundred yards behind the barn. Can you dump the weapons there? He has a tractor and will fill it in once we leave."

Without speaking, Austin and Mikeis moved toward the barn door.

"Oh, and wash them with bleach first," Ron said as he pointed toward a bottle of cleaning solution in the corner. Mikeis jogged over and grabbed the bottle before following Austin outside. After a minute, the rest of the men trickled outside and stripped off their jumpsuits. Jack held out a black trash bag for each man to deposit his uniform and rabbit mask into as they walked by. Slowly, the men piled into their cars and back down the driveway before disappearing over the hill. After a few minutes, Ron and Jack were the only two left.

"You good?" Jack asked.

Ron shook his head. "I'll never be good again." Ron could hear the faint echo of sirens heading toward the cabin.

"You think we got away with it?" Jack asked.

Ron nodded. "As long as you can burn those uniforms without getting caught."

"Won't be an issue. Every officer in the county is rushing toward that cabin," Jack said, pointing out the enormous cloud of smoke in the distance. "I'm heading that way." Jack pointed in the opposite direction. Jack shook his head and stuck out his hand. "Thanks for everything."

Ron shook it. "Sure, Jack."

Jack tossed the black trash bag into the back seat of his truck and climbed into the driver's seat. He gave Ron his last nod and drove off. Ron leaned against the wall and watched him disappear over the hill before going back into the barn.

Ron walked up to the poker table and poured the vodka into one of the shot glasses. He slid himself down into a seat and retrieved a half-smoked cigar from the ashtray at the center of the table. He clenched the end of the cigar between his teeth. Grabbing the lighter off the table, he sparked the end and puffed on the cigar until the opposite end burned a deep shade of orange. He dug in his pocket and fished out a picture of his daughter. Laying it flat on the table, he looked at it for a moment before tossing back the shot of vodka. A burning sensation rushed down his throat and spread across his chest. He smacked his lips together and rested a hand on the photograph.

"I'm sorry, sweet girl." Tears streamed down his face now. "I couldn't protect you, but I made damn sure those monsters would never hurt anyone again." His hand slid the picture to the edge of the table. Slowly, he folded the picture in half again and returned it to his pocket. He tossed the still-smoking cigar into the ashtray and walked outside. As he walked across the field that lay between his house and the barn, he watched the large plume of black smoke rising in the distance. The sound of sirens echoed from all directions.

Ron patted the pocket that had the picture of his little girl and smiled.

About the Author

Timothy King is an adult horror author who enjoys delving into the complexities of human nature. He also narrates audiobooks under the pen name TC King. When he is not writing spine-chilling tales, he is spending time with his wife and kids in beautiful Tampa, Florida.

You can find him on Facebook, Tiktok or by emailing him at:

Timothykingauthor@gmail.com

If you enjoyed this book, please consider leaving a review on Amazon or Goodreads!

Other works:

In Progress:

A novella the Author is classifying as a "Cult Horror Romance."

Completed Audiobook narration:

Timothy narrated "Mine" By LM Kaplin, under his pen name TC King. This audiobook is available on Audible.

Printed in Great Britain
by Amazon

45994578R00118